COBALT

AISHA BUFORD-MORRISON

COBALT

Author: Aisha Buford-Morrison

ISBN- 978-0692140666

ISBN- 0692140662

LCCN: TBD

Editing/Typesetting/Bookcover: Young Dreams Publications

Connect with Aisha Buford-Morrison

theauthoraisha@gmail.com

Twitter: @theauthoraisha

Instagram: theauthoraisha

Dedication

To my future children, I have worked so hard to accomplish my dreams so that you can go after yours. You are your mother's child (ren) - for God only knows - and saying that life is too hard will not work for me. I've chased my dream at a young age with a learning disability, go after yours.

Acknowledgments

Thank you to my fabulous editors. Also my biggest supporters, Lori and Mom. I couldn't have done this without you two helping me along the way. Thank you, Cartez for lending your artist's eye and helping me chose the color scheme for the cover of the book.

About the Author

 I am Aisha Buford-Morrison, a 19-year-old African American woman from the South Side of Chicago. I graduated from Epic Academy Charter High School in 2016. I published my first novel, *Heart Be Still*, on Valentine's Day 2018. I would have never thought that at 19 years old I would have self-published two books. I have been writing short stories since my young adolescent's age. I never let my learning disability (dyslexia) stop me from accomplishing my dreams. I would have never imagined that one day I would have books of my own. My books are something that I will always hold deep to my heart. I am Aisha Buford-Morrison, enjoy reading my books.

Black We Can

Little black girl hold your head up high

You are a descendant of an African queen

Little black boy you are a prince becoming a king

You are not a thug

You are not a criminal

Your thick curly hair resembles God

You move with grace and tranquility

Little black girl and boy don't you cry

You are not a slave

You are not oppressed

You are not broken

You are magical

You are strong

You are free

Blackbird

Dear Diary,

I'm having a hard time lately. It's been a minute since I had any thoughts worth writing down. The last three months without my mom have been the worst. My life revolved around her. When she was alive, we were inseparable. It's not like I didn't know she was going to die, it's still getting harder not having her here with me to guide me. I don't think it will ever get easy for me to be without her. The good thing about her being gone is that she's not suffering from cancer anymore. My mom fought a long battle with stage 4 breast cancer. Still, it's hard watching the very woman who gave birth to you not be able to take care of herself.

When she was alive, I remember her just lying in bed waiting to die. My dad is the only parent that I have left. I don't see him as my parent. Even when my mom was here his preferred method of communication to me is through text messages. All my life he has put me on hold. The only thing that made this house a home was my mom.

All summer I took care of her all the way up until the very end. Today is the first day of school, and I'm trying to convince myself that this year will be okay. I should be heading to school, but instead, I'm sitting in a cemetery sitting up against a tree writing while looking at my mother's headstone. She's about to miss out on my senior year of high school. Every year that I have been in school, she would have taken a picture of me. I used to get so annoyed every first day that she would do it. I'd give anything to have her do it one more time. Well let me head to school, I'll write you later.

~Amara

I woke up extra early today to see my mom. I think it's weird that I like talking to her even though she can't respond back to me. Oddly, yet I find it comforting to speak to her spirit. My dad is suffering inside without my mom. His grief has turned him into a functioning alcoholic. Every day he goes to work then comes home and kills a case or two of beer, and then passes out at seven.

My mom's death has disrupted our regular pattern of life. I'm struggling to find hope that this year will be a breeze. I'm being optimistic that my mom not being here won't affect me much, but who am I kidding, I'm sure it probably will.

I need to get out more and stop the anti-social behavior that I've been displaying as of late. It's time for me to enter back into the world and get on with my life. My friends understand why I have been missing for the last couple of months. Considering how we live in a tiny town in the middle of nowhere I didn't miss much. I walked like a turtle to school – slow, very freaking slow. There's a part of me that wants to run and hide and try again next year. I've actually been out of school for a while. I finished my junior early because of what happened with my mom – the counselors agreed that it was better that I wrap up the school year and focus on my mental health and mourning. As I went on my way to school, the more I walked, the more my stomach started to ball up into a knot. It's just school, I thought to myself. I don't know why I'm so nervous. Cars filled with students and their parents zipped by me as I felt like I was moving in slow motion. As I'm walking down the street, a truck abruptly stops and pulls over to the side.

"Hey, haven't seen you in forever! Amara do you want a ride to school?" Zhivago says yelling out of the window.

"Zhivago, nice to see you. Thanks, I'm good I can use the air." I say swooping some of my hair behind my ears.

"Oh come on, after knowing me for six years you can't let me take you to school? Come on Amara hop in the car." He says opening the truck door.

"Fine..." I roll my eyes while getting into the truck.

I didn't put up much of a fight with Zhivago. Sometimes it's better to go with the flow and get things over with so you can move on. I get in Zhivago's raggedy truck, it was so old I swear it was getting ready to fall apart any second. His vehicle used to be red, but now it has taken on the shade of light pink. The seats are covered in patches in an attempt to repair the holes in the upholstery. He needed to get rid of this truck two centuries ago, along with the old eighties music he likes to listen to. And let's not talk about the rust, the amount of rust that this truck has accumulated is unbelievable. As we journey the rest of the way to school, I just look out the window watching the birds fly away.

We pull up into the parking lot of Barker High School, and it feels like I have never been here. So much has changed in such little time. Zhivago pulls up to the parking space right next to all our friends who look like they were waiting for us. While everyone seemed so refreshed from summer, I looked like I was a zombie. It's weird seeing everyone acting as if nothing happened at the end of last year. Tess was, of course, doing her makeup as always. She wants to be the most beautiful girl that has ever walked the earth. Tess is one of the most feminine girls I have ever known. Her mouth gets her into a lot of fights. She has no problem hurting other's feelings. If you were to compare us to one another, I'm the complete opposite of her.

I have long, thick, curly black hair that reaches the middle of my back when stretched. My face is round. I have horrible acne scars all over. And let's not forget about the discoloration in my skin. Since my skin is the shade of cappuccino, I tend to scar more easily. I wear a size sixteen in jeans. I'm very curvy - not the skinniest girl. And I love listening to classical music. Funny, I can't tell you how many times I have been called a nerd. My life is as dull as it could be. Every guy at school wants Tess, and she enjoys that, and I'm happy for her. I might be a little jealous of her sometimes, that's because nothing wrong ever happens to her. Tess has a perfect life for right now. Her boyfriend is Jonny, the star of the baseball team. He's very tall and skinny. They will break up before you know it. I don't expect much to come from their relationship. Tess goes through guys like water. High school love is not meant to last if you ask me.

Anne was sitting on the ground listening to her music zoned out not paying any attention to us. She looks good, still hasn't outgrown her punk rock phase and has dyed her hair blue. Eric and Ethan were too busy playing football to care what we were doing. Everyone was asking me how I was doing just to be polite. I just wanted to forget the last three months of my life. School right now will be giving me time to escape the issues going on at home. A little ordinary would do some good for me right now.

We all sat outside waiting for the first-period warning bell to ring. Today is going to be a good day - I repeated in my head as I walked to first period with Zhivago. The one thing about living in a small town is that we all know each other. Word was spreading fast that there was a new guy. Honestly, who cares if there's a new student here? It's almost like we're in the first grade, and everyone is happy about the new shiny toy. I probably won't meet the new guy anyway.

As I miserably work my way to biology class, I dread the idea of sitting through the class. One thing I hate about school is the assigned seats. I can't wait to go to college and experience the more independent life of education. And also biology is the worst class created in the history of learning. Learning about how all living organisms work like anything living won't die anyway – maybe I'm still jaded because of the death of my mom. I think the course should be renamed to "Please kill me I'm dying of boredom." I don't know, I'm just not feeling it, but at least the teacher seems fun. Ms. Hoven graduated at the top of her college class. She has very tan skin with fire red hair. As we walk through the door, she cracks corny jokes while giving us our assigned seat locations. She places Zhivago to the front of the class because he is the class clown – she must have been given a head's up from all of our previous teachers from last year. I am most elated when I find out my seat is at the back of the class. Every year I ask to sit in the front of the class, but this year I wanted to stay as far in the back as possible.

I sit in the back of the room and wait for class to start. Everyone who I walk pass looks so happy, ready to start senior year. Shortly, after everyone piles in, the new kid walks into the classroom. I stare at everyone when the new kid walks into the room – I was curious to see the reactions as he was already such a big deal before anyone even knew who he was. It's a shame that our town is so small that we recognize a new face so easily, that's how everyone knew he was the new kid. Everyone starts whispering under their breath about him. He must be about six-feet tall, 190 pounds. His hair was short black and was cut low with waves. His eyes were black-brown, and his skin was dark. He was wearing a grey shirt, black pants, and gym shoes. Even with him being the new kid he walks in with confidence - intriguing. Ms. Hoven instructs him that his seat for the year was next to me. I tried to act like I didn't even notice him, I start taking out paper and other standard supplies to look like I was busy. Zhivago saw the fresh kid walking over to me and bolts over to me to feel what type of person he is. Male jealousy I take it, because Zhivago doesn't always make friends quickly.

"So, you look like the new kid everyone has been talking about? You look like you play football for a living." Zhivago says laughing.

"Well, I assure you I'm not a football player. Otherwise, I wouldn't be here in class. I would be making millions somewhere." He says with a straight face.

"Zhivago leave him alone. Go sit down, it's too early in the morning for you to be starting anything." I say examining the class syllabus.

"Just for your love, I'll go sit down. I will be watching you, dude." He laughs and walks away.

The rule of making a great first impression applies throughout life, and I think Zhivago just failed this one. It's almost like he doesn't understand that you can't just walk up to anyone and say what you feel. Now Zhivago has put me in an awkward position to try and fix the mess he has created all by himself while throwing me in the sinking ship. I watch Zhivago walk back to the front of the room. I look at him like he was a complete idiot.

"I'm sorry, he's a weird idiot." I say hoping that it will make up for Zhivago being rude to him.

"Your boyfriend is a little overprotective of you." He looks at me dead in my eyes.

"He is not my boyfriend, and I'm not dating anyone. It's a small town we have known each other for a couple of years. I treat him like he's my annoying brother. We are nothing more than just friends." I say quickly.

"Okay, well your friend is protective of you. You don't have to apologize for him. I didn't get a chance to introduce myself, yet. I'm Jabari." He smiles.

I'm intrigued even the more. "I'm Amara, or Mara, for short." I smile back harder.

"That's a beautiful name, Amara." He grins looking down at my hands balled in a fist.

Jabari and I are distracted by Ms. Hoven starting to crack jokes attempting to get everyone excited about the new school year. It's school, I'm forced to wake up every day and come here, at least she's trying to understand our pain. I was starting to have a good day until she gave the class our first partner project. She just stuck the knife into my heart and twisted it without even knowing. I'm pretty sure there are a thousand different topics she could have chosen. Why did she have to choose cancer? I thought today would be a good day, but I see that it's going entirely left. I thought I was going to have a panic attack in class. It's just the pain of losing my mother hasn't stopped yet, and my home life is a wreck because of it. Jabari could kind of sense my uneasiness, but he didn't say anything, and I wasn't going to say anything either. Hearing the word cancer just wholly fries my brain. And doing a partner assignment on it is not going to help.

Hearing the bell ring for the next class was the best thing in the world. Before walking out of biology, I gave him my number. We will have to meet up in the next couple of days to start working on the research project. I don't know about Jabari, but I have seen the results first hand, and they're not good. The question I have for myself is will I be able to get through this assignment smoothly and remaining sane.

Time was moving so fast today I thought someone was doing time magic because I could believe it was lunchtime already. I wasn't interested in eating and hanging out with everyone, so I went by my locker and sat on the school hallway floor. There was no point in trying to act like I was okay. I pull out my journal and start drawing in it, that's what I usually do when I'm a little stressed.

As I'm journaling a bit, I happen to look up and see Jabari staring at me. He snuck up on me while I wasn't looking. It was weird because I didn't know how long he'd been there watching me. I jump when I see him. "Ah, you scared the hell out of me."

"Sorry, didn't mean to scare you. Why are you sitting out here by yourself? I'm the one with no friends." He says smiling at me.

"That's solely because you're new to the school. Most of us grew up together. Jabari, you will make friends soon. But I don't mean to be anti-social, but I got a lot on my mind." I say.

"Well since you're the only person I know do you mind if I sit?" He says.

"Sure, go ahead."

We sat on the floor and just talk. Jabari was from a big city up north. His mother thought it would be good for him to move down here to learn more about their family history. Jabari also wanted to know more about me, but there wasn't that much to tell. He has experienced more life than I have, coming from a big city where there are a lot more things to do than just play in the woods. Jabari did get my mind off everything for a while. He asks if we could meet after school to come up with a game plan. The bell rings and he helped me off the floor. I tell him to meet me at my locker after school so we could sit at Fred's grill and work on it. Fred's was like a second home seeing that my mom used to work there before she died. They will let us sit in there for as long as we want.

At the end of the day, as promised, Jabari was standing by my locker waiting for me. I grab all my things, and we walk out together. Usually, I wouldn't get into a car with someone I just met, but I don't feel like walking, so I'm willing to take the risk. The only thing I want to do is go to the cemetery before the evening is over with. Since she's gone, I need to see her grave every single day to get used to her not being around. I know that doesn't make much sense, but that's my coping mechanism. I zone out in the car; he plays a punk rock song that was pretty good. Usually, I'm able to read people and understand what type of person they are. For some reason with him, I can't seem to. I instruct Jabari on how to get to Fred's. The drive there was quick.

Fred's Grill was a great place for me, from the time I was a very small girl I always had memories of my mom working there. Every time I come and visit it reminds me of her. Other than the fact that this is where my mother worked, it's a regular old diner. Hayden was our waitress for the night, she seated us towards the back of the restaurant. She also made it completely weird for me, seeing how I have never been a date in my young life. Hayden believes that Jabari and I are out on a date. She not the type of person to make things not so obvious which is good. As we place our order, she looks me in my eye and smirks as she walks away.

"So, I was thinking we could do a slide show about how cancer affects the human body. Ms. Hoven gave everyone free creative range on presenting." I say pulling my notebook out my bag.

"Sure, we can split up the work. You can research the effects cancer has on the families of the patients. I can research on what cancer does to the body at each stage." He says looking at me.

"Yeah sure." I struggle to try to say because I felt uncomfortable.

I wrote down each of our roles in the project. I try every single day not to be weird, and somehow I fail to do that. Hayden came back to the table with our food, we put off homework for a little bit. Hayden had a twinkle in her eyes when she sits the food down on the table. She swishes away back to the front of the restaurant.

Just when the conversation was going great, and I was having fun, my dad comes into the restaurant drunk looking for my mom. He starts fighting with some of the restaurant staff. Out of all nights, why did he have to get so drunk that he starts a fight? I don't ask for much in life, the only thing I wanted was to do my homework and call it a day. Now I must deal with the drunkenness of my blundering father. I run over to him while was he's punching Manny the dishwasher in the face screaming my mom's name. I tell my dad to stop. He turns from Manny and picks up a bottle and hits me in the head with it. I fall to the floor with a bloodied gash on my forehead. I'm utterly embarrassed that everyone is witnessing what is happening. As I get up off the ground, a couple of guys grab hold of my dad and holds him back. I put my hand on his face and scream to tell my dad that my mom is dead. He stops his drunken rage dropping to the floor crying. I grab the keys out of his pocket, run to the table were Jabari was sitting and gather my things. I could barely look Jabari in the eye. I left enough money on the table to pay for the meal and left.

My dad is now passed out drunk when we both arrived at the house. I help him upstairs to his bedroom and leave him. I could die tonight and be happy. There was a small piece of glass stuck in my forehead that I couldn't get out. I struggle for ten minutes digging into my forehead trying to wedge the glass out. I was upstairs in the bathroom when I hear a knock on the door. I figured someone called the police on my dad. I proceed to open the door, and it was Jabari.

"Hey." I say shocked.

"Hey, I don't want you to think that I'm stalking you or anything. You were in such a rush to get out of there you left your journal. I figured I'd bring this back to you, so here." He says handing the journal over.

"Thanks, I didn't even realize that I left it. How did you find me?" I say taking my journal from him.

"Small town. I ask the waitress where you lived. Don't worry I didn't read anything." He awkwardly grins.

"Oh, thank you again! I'm sorry about tonight. You didn't need to see any of that." I glance at the ground.

"You don't have to apologize. Mara, you did nothing wrong. It looks like you have a bad gash on your head. I can help you if you need it?" He says.

"Thanks, I don't think I need help with it." I say quickly. I sit and think or a second. "Who am I kidding, I do need your help. There's a piece of glass stuck in my forehead. I can't seem to get it out." I pause and plead for his help.

"Okay." He beams and walks into my house.

I went up to the bathroom and brought down the tweezers off the sink counter. Jabari instructs me to hold onto him as he digs around in my bloody wound to get the glass out. Luckily Jabari was pretty buff and could handle me squeezing his right side. He pulls the piece of the beer bottle out of my forehead. I couldn't thank him enough for being able to retrieve the glass. After he removes the glass from my forehead, he places a Band-Aid on my wound and leaves. I watch him drive away through the window in the living room. I run up to my room and change into my evening clothes and quickly grab my journal.

Dear Diary:

Remember when I told you this morning that I was going to have a fantastic school year. Well, I ultimately take back that statement. I barely even know Jabari, and my dad attacks Manny at Fred's and then ends up hitting me in the head with a beer bottle. That's an excellent way to get to know someone. I like old school rap, swimming, and oh yeah, my father is a drunk. He just made us look like a messed up family, which I do not deny we are not the perfect family.

I didn't even realize that I left my journal at the table. Makes sense to me because I was too busy trying to save face. At least Jabari doesn't seem too weirded out by it. I want to know what my mom would say to me right now if she were here. Now I have to figure out how to make it up to Jabari.

~Amara

Consciousness

I have been hanging out with Jabari a lot lately because of our project. He's brilliant and funny. I've been trying to make up to him for the debacle at Fred's. The first time you meet me and my dad goes on a drunken rampage, and you have to help me get a broken piece of glass out of my head.

I still have been eating lunch at my locker and Jabari has been joining me. He seems to be the type of person to stick to himself. It's nice to have someone who doesn't know your whole life story. Here in the town of Peter, everyone knows what goes on in your life. I want to get away and escape this town. If I were Jabari, I would have chosen to stay in the city. There are so many people no one has time to worry about you. I sit by my locker as usual during lunch and eat my sandwich while I work on my homework. Jabari soon joins me halfway through our lunch period.

"I thought you were skipping out on me today." I snicker.

"No, I just went for a run for a bit. I needed to blow off some steam." He says sitting down next to me.

"Blowing off some steam? Are you okay?" I ask.

"I have had some built up tension, so I figured the best thing for me to do is to run it all off, that's all. I did want to ask you something." He says sliding down the lockers.

"Sure, what is it?"

"Considering how we have been spending so much time together, you know working on our project. I was wondering if you would like to go to the movies on Saturday? There's a movie called *Flowers* being shown at the drive-in movie theater. It's a movie from the early 80's, and it's a black and white film. Not forcing you but if you're free would you like to come?" Jabari asks trying to persuade me.

"Are you asking me on a date?" I blush.

"I can see you saw through my plan of taking you out. Yes, I'm asking you out." He laughs.

"Yes, I would love to." I respond right in time for our lunch period to end.

I don't know what to think of him asking me out. The one thing I notice is that being around Jabari makes me smile a lot. I was walking to my next class writing in my notebook not paying attention to where I was going. The one thing about me is that when I'm in my own world, I stay there. I was busy writing in my journal. I didn't even see myself running right into Zhivago. I kind of have been avoiding most of my friends. Since my mom died, they're always trying to make sure I'm okay, and it's starting to get annoying. Jabari hasn't asked about her. I like that he doesn't know anything about me. It makes me feel free.

"Sorry, Zhivago I didn't see you there," I say bending over to pick up my books.

"It's okay! Hey Amara, do you want to hang out Saturday?" Zhivago asks.

"Zhivago, sorry Jabari already asked me out this weekend." I say looking at him as he begins to pout at the news.

"Jabari? Do you even know anything about him?" He shouts.

"I know enough. You're jealous of him, aren't you?" I say punching him in his arm giggling at him.

"No, I'm not! I want to make sure you're going to be okay that's all. Just be careful." He says.

I take his concerns into consideration, but I really don't think I have much to worry about.

Saturday night rolls around. I was actually looking forward to our date. I realize that I always ask Jabari questions about himself, but I change the subject when he tries to find things out about me. There's nothing much to me. I think I live a pretty bland life. In my eyes, nothing is exciting about me. Whatever he sees in me I have no idea. I pray that we have a perfect night. The last thing I need is for my dad to have a break down again. I think it might be safe to say that we will have a good night tonight.

I sit in the kitchen waiting for Jabari to pick me up. My dad was passed out drunk on the couch. I still wonder how his body hasn't given out yet from drinking all the time. I'm sort of disgusted with him. I know that mom died, but that doesn't mean you get to stop trying to live. Jabari pulls up to the front of my house and he honks his horn. I grab my bag and head for the door. I was wearing jeans and my favorite blue cat shirt. I made sure that the house was locked up. My father has been so intoxicated as of late, he's starting to have the bad habit of leaving the door unlocked. Soon someone will realize that the door will be open and rob us.

After I lock the door and turn around Jabari was standing by the passenger's door waiting on me to come to the car.

"After you, my lady." He says smiling.

"Thank you! I take it no one ever told you that chivalry is dead." I say while getting in the car.

"Chivalry is not dead with me." He smiles closing the door.

It's weird being on my first date with someone. Jabari and I have been alone with each other before, but the circumstances were different and it didn't feel so intimate. But we have been together with other people around. I'm comfortable with being alone with him, so I'm not afraid. It's just that I can tell that he likes me and I feel like I'm damaged goods. I'm not the type of girl you bring home to your mother – I think. I have a lot of baggage that's weighing me down. My mother is dead, and my father's a drunk. In the house I'm pretty much alone, I take care of myself. I'm close to going insane.

Jabari gets popcorn and gummies for us to snack on. The movie Jabari picks is pretty good. *Flowers* is about a girl who helplessly falls in love with a guy who just enlisted in the war. Eventually, the guy gets sent off to fight for the country and dies while fighting on the front lines. He leaves the woman he loves broken beyond repair and lost without him. During most of the movie we half watch and talk more than usual.

"So, can I ask why you wanted to go out with me?" I say snacking on popcorn.

"You make it sound like it was a horrible decision to ask you out, Amara." He says looking at me popping popcorn in his mouth and chewing loudly.

"Well look at me. I wouldn't be my first pick for someone to go out with. I mean, look at me." I say staring at his huge black eyes.

"I see nothing wrong with you. I only see a beautiful girl in front of me. What do you think I see when I look at you?" He says.

"I think you see a girl whose dad is a drunk. A girl who's overweight and dresses in sweatpants every day. A girl who is too lazy to do her hair every day, so she either slaps it in a ponytail or puts it in cornrows. I'm a girl so devoted to school that I rather do homework than hang out with friends." I say.

As I was going on my tangent Jabari kisses me, I guess to shut me up. I should have probably slapped him for doing that, but I didn't. He kisses me then pulls back looking at me in my eyes. I didn't know how to feel, my heart was pounding so loud I couldn't hear my brain thinking.

"I like what I see when I'm looking at you." He says..

"Oh." I say not knowing how to react to the kiss.

After he kisses me, we continue to watch the movie. In my head, I was still trying to figure out how to process everything. I don't know how to handle all this new information. Things are happening so fast for me. Why would he kiss me like that? I had to remind myself to relax and not get too happy about anything.

The movie ends, and Jabari is driving me home when he gets a call from his grandmother. He starts talking in a different language, I couldn't make out what he was saying. The conversation sounds like nothing but gibberish. He hangs up the phone and turns to look at me.

"Hey, I need to run to my house before dropping you off. My grandmother needs help. It sounds urgent. After I help her I will drop you off at home. I'm sorry!" He says making sure that I would be okay with the change.

He made a sharp right turn at the end of the road. I have never been on this road before. There were barely any lights on the path. Jabari pulls up to his home and lets me come inside to wait until he's done helping his grandmother. The house was decorated entirely in African prints and lions. He leaves me in the living room and goes to see where his grandmother is.

I walk around in the living room looking over some of the decorations in the room. A lot of the artifacts are beautiful. This is my culture, I say to myself as I think about it. Sadly, I also realize I don't know anything about it. Jabari comes back downstairs to the living room after helping his grandmother. I am standing in the front of the coffee table stationed in the middle of the room.

"I see your grandmother likes lions a lot." I say walking over to a massive painting of a lion on the wall.

"My family is from Tanzania, so she has a lot of things that remind her of Africa." He says walking up behind me.

"That still doesn't explain the lions, am I missing something?" I say looking confused.

"Well, when our ancestors lived in Africa we were rulers. We had the greatest empire known to man. That all changed once slavery happened. Our loved ones were stolen away from us. They were trapped like animals. Have you ever heard of the Tau tribe?" He says staring at me.

"No." I say looking at some of the lions and tribal artifacts.

"Well, that's my families' tribe if you will. They used to live in the Shari Desert, and supposedly we are descended from lions." He says picking up one of the lions.

"Lions?! Like actual kill a zebra, lion?" I laugh.

"Yes, which is why my grandparents have all the lions everywhere. Growing up my grandmother used to tell me how the men of the tribe would go out, hunt, and bring back food for the village. The women made basket, clothes, and took care of the kids. When slavery happened, they invaded the village, killed, and took as many people as they could. The men of the tribe were shape-shifters that could transform into lions and tried to take out as many as they could. They had guns, and some were shot down. The Tau leader sacrificed his life and took out the lead general who was leading the people into captivity. He died trying to save the people of the tribe. Everyone else ran trying to flee as quickly as possible. Trying not to be enslaved." He says looking at the painting.

"Wow, that's heartbreaking to hear. You know it always bothered me not knowing where my origin started. I'm kind of jealous of you. Why haven't I ever heard about it before?" I say looking at him.

"It's not your fault that you don't know about the shape-shifting tribe, but really it's the same reason why you never hear about a lot of African history after colonization. It's funny how we are the first to create civilization but were somehow colonized." Jabari looks around and grabs his keys. "Well, I'm finished helping my grandmother. I can take you home now." He says glancing over at the door.

During the car ride home, I couldn't help but think about what my life would have been like if my mom was still here. I'm getting tired of having to take care of my dad. He needs help, and I don't think that anyone other than me realizes how bad off he is. I say goodnight to Jabari and go up to my room. My dad was most likely gone to the bar.

Dear Diary:

Jabari is amazing. He seems to be interested in me. I don't see why he would be. I'm no one special. He kissed me, and I don't know how to feel about that. I mean, we have been hanging out with each other a lot. I guess he fell in love with me. Or whatever love is at our age. I can't seem to get him out of my head. Am I in love with him? I am in love with him. I don't want to get my hopes up I'll have to take my time with this. He could be trying to feel me out to see if I'm into him. I have never put this much trust into anyone before. It's been a long time since I have felt like I could put my faith into someone like this again.

~Amara

Lion Walking In The Dessert

I guess it's safe to say that Jabari and I might be in a relationship. As of late, we haven't been focusing on our project. We are more interested in each other. Zhivago is jealous of Jabari. Guys aren't the best at trying to hide their emotions like girls. Every time he sees Jabari and me together he starts acting like a kid. I don't know what has gotten into him as of late. It could be that I haven't been hanging out with him anyone. I'm trying to make it through the year by not being anti-social so I suggest to Jabari that we eat lunch with my friends. I even suggest that this would be a great opportunity for him to make new friends other me.

"Look who decided to join us for lunch. What? You're not hiding today?" Tess says picking up a chip.

"It feels weird having you sit with us again. You have been eating lunch all by yourself since school started. What has made the great Amara social again?" Eric laughs, almost choking on his food.

"I haven't been eating alone every day. Jabari found me sitting by myself at the lockers on the first day. Since then he has been eating with me. He should be coming over here soon." I say grabbing a seat.

"Aw, Mara is falling in love. Amara and Jabari sounds good together." Anne says making fun of me.

"We're not together. We are just hanging out with each other. Whatever the future holds for me I'll have to wait and see just like you." I say as I bend over pulling my lunch out of my bag.

"Well, I think that you two will be together." Tess says while reaching to hold Jonny's hand.

"I don't think he's good for you anyway, Amara!" Zhivago says looking upset.

"You're only saying that because she will never give you a chance." Anne laughs.

"That's not funny, Anne." I say rolling my eyes at her.

Anne doesn't always know the right things to say to everyone. I could tell right away that Zhivago was very uncomfortable with what she says. I turn around to see if Jabari was in the cafeteria. When I turn around, we lock eyes. I was looking for my quickest way out of this situation. Sadly, there was no window for me to jump out. Jabari walks over confidently and seems tense. He grabs the chair next to me sitting and smiling at me awkwardly. Somehow looking into his eyes makes me forget about everything that's going on in my life. There's just something about him that takes all the pain away from me.

Tess just watches us looking at each other being typical teenagers. My friends haven't seen much of him. He's distant with everyone besides me. Tess is like an animal stalking its prey as she waits before she goes in for the kill.

"So, Jabari I see you have been hanging out with Amara a lot. I take it you like her?" Zhivago says.

"Yes, she's amazing." He says looking at me which makes me smile.

"Well, you don't know anything about her. I have grown up with her, and I know more than you, dude." Zhivago says staring at Jabari.

"Okay, and your point is what exactly?" Jabari says looking confused.

"You don't know anything about her. I bet she didn't tell you about the time she went swimming about almost drowned. Or like that time she got stuck on the Ferris wheel. She panicked crying to get out. I bet she didn't tell you about her mom." Zhivago says happily and enthusiast.

"That's enough you ass! Don't you dare bring up my mother again. Do you hear me?" I get up and leave the lunchroom wanting to fight Zhivago.

Zhivago is starting to piss me off. He has no right to use me to try and prove to Jabari that he is better than him. My mother is still a sensitive topic for me to talk about. I left the lunchroom pissed. It's only been months since she left this earth, not even a full year yet. He thinks he can just bring it up as a joke. Who does that to someone that you call a friend? I go and sit by my locker to finish up the lunch period. I sit on the floor just pondering. Zhivago should know my rule. I don't mix friendships like that. There is only something about Jabari that might make me reconsider that rule. Zhivago is like a brother to me and nothing more. I was alone for probably a little under fifteen minutes before Jabari comes and finds me. Honestly, it was an easy guess.

"Are you okay?" Jabari asks standing over me.

"A little pissed off, but I'm good. I'm glad you came after me we kind of need to talk." I say looking up at him.

"I think I know where this is going." He walks over to the window and leans his back up against it.

"The kiss. What does that mean for us now?" I say scared to ask shrugging my shoulders.

"The kiss meant that I want you to be my girlfriend. I think you're an amazing girl and I like you. We have been spending a lot of time together, and I'm feeling you." He says looking at me leaning up against the window.

"Oh... I was afraid of that." I say looking up from my notebook.

"Why would you say that? You're amazing." He says moving closer to me.

"I'm like an old car. I'm only good until all my parts start breaking. You will have me around until you see how broken down I am." I explain.

"Well, I have rebuilt an engine for a 1971 van before. I like you, so I'm up for the challenge if you're willing to give me a chance. Whatever happens, we will go with the flow." He says sliding down to the floor.

Jabari has a way of making me feel that I'm able to trust him. I have never been the type to move fast with a relationships – heck, I've never been in a relationship I think and begin to laugh at myself. I should be taking things slow, but my heart is speaking louder than my brain. Sometimes you must walk through mud to walk on solid ground. The bell rings. He kisses me and we go our separate ways. I watch him walk away. Have you ever felt like you were walking on a cloud? That's exactly how I feel with Jabari - weightless.

The weeks go by, Jabari and I have been hanging out almost every single day. We are learning more about each other. Fred's has become our hang out spot. I'm starting to be able to admit to myself that I like him. Maybe even love him. Also, Jabari has been teaching me how to speak Zulu. I suck at it, but he's helping. We were at Fred's when Zhivago comes in and sits at the table with us. It's like he feels that he needs to be all in my space. Zhivago starts grabbing my hand and kissing it. As he's kissing my hand and I'm trying to pull away, Jabari tells him to stop.

Zhivago gives him a look and ignores him. Jabari stands up ready to fight Zhivago. I snatch my hand away quickly and stand up just as Zhivago stands. I brace my body between them hoping to divert the fight that appears to be ready to kick off. I turn and look at Jabari, he grabs his stuff and leaves. I shove Zhivago out the way to runs after Jabari, but when I get outside he was driving away.

I'm not sure what made Jabari so upset but he begins to ignore me ever since the incident with Zhivago. I try to call Jabari every day, but he hasn't been picking up. I have called him so much that I have memorized his voice mail message. I have only been to his grandparents' house once, so I don't exactly know where he lives. What makes things worst is that our project is due this week and I don't know if he's coming to school or not. He hasn't been to school in a couple of weeks.

It is Tuesday and I was standing by my locker getting my books for the day. I look over my shoulders and lock eyes with Jabari. The missing him feeling I had left entirely and was replaced with anger and hurt. I think I was feeling more hurt than anything else. He walks over to me with a sad look on his face.

"Hey, Amara. Can we talk?" Jabari walks up to me switching out my books and placing them in the locker for me.

"I don't feel like talking to you." I say trying to find my notebook for Biology.

"Amara, let me explain." Jabari tries to plead his case.

"You ask me to be your girlfriend, and then you stop returning my calls. It's been a couple of weeks since you been to school. Jabari, you dropped off the face of the earth. What Zhivago did was wrong, but you could have at least returned my calls." I stop frantically searching for my notebook and look at him.

"I can explain everything if you let me. I just need you to give me a chance." He jumps in front of me.

"Save it. It's my fault for getting my hopes up that someone would like me for a change. I believed you. I started to fall in love with you. Thanks for taking the little piece of hope away from me. I'll see you in class." I say looking at Jabari.

I walk away from Jabari feeling disappointed in myself. Jabari was starting to make me forget about all my problems at home. Never put your trust so deep into someone. Not everyone that comes into your life is here to stay. It doesn't help that I have a class with him next and we just broke up.

I'm in my seat waiting for class to start trying to push away all of my emotions so that I can present the project properly. I go over some notes I had written down for the presentation. Breaking

up with Jabari and having to present with him is going to be weird.

I don't know how to feel about everything. I think I'm just hurt.

Jabari comes into class and sits right next to me. I'm just hoping

that he completed his part of the project.

"Class, take your seats. Now as you all know today is the

day you present your project about cancer to the class. Let's see

who is first on my class roster. Amara and Jabari looks like you

two are up first." Ms. Hoven says.

We walk up to the front of the classroom and stand next to

the big screen on the wall. Jabari and I look awkward standing next

to each other. Almost like we're meeting for the first time. Jabari

looks at me and then starts to go over the research he did for his

assignment. Then the slide turns to my portion of the presentation.

The slide changes to a picture of my mother.

"The woman you see behind me is my mother. She died of

breast cancer some months ago. Cancer doesn't just affect the

person with the illness, it affects their family. For months I saw life

being stripped out of my mother. We were no longer mother and daughter; I became her nurse. I held her cold frail hand as she took her last breath on this earth. That memory is forever imprinted in my mind. I will live the rest of my life without my mother." I say choking and holding back my tears.

After I was done talking no one clapped for us. The room was dead silent you could hear everyone's hair growing out of their scalp. I walk back to my seat and look for the next person to go up. I could see Jabari out of the corner of my eye looking at me. I folded back into my seat not paying attention to anything that was going on in class. My emotions were all over the place. I watch the clock countdown to next period. I grab my stuff and run out of the room as soon as the bell rings.

"Hey Amara, wait up!" Zhivago says running after me.

"Oh, hey, Zhivago!" I say walking fast.

"Are you alright? I know that was hard for you to do." He jumps in front of me stopping me.

"I'm fine, I guess." I say even though a part of me wasn't.

"A bunch of us are throwing a bond fire party this Saturday at the beach. Do you want to come? After today you could use some fun." Zhivago says smiling.

"Sure. I'm having a crappy week." I say forcing myself to speak.

I glance over and see Jabari staring at me. This week is starting to be horrible. I don't think that anything can get worse than today. I'm hurt, not like an average hurt. I feel like I'm in pain right now, death would be the best thing for me. I started falling for Jabari. There is nothing worse than dying from a broken heart.

The day moved on with everyone shuffling through the halls laughing, while I look like a wild animal attacked me. The bags under my eyes are growing each day. Each day it seems like I have been losing more sleep than what I should.

Today I just want to be alone. When lunch comes around instead of eating by my locker, I go outside. I sit on the old red bench that could use a paint job. I look around hopelessly trying to figure out what to do with my life. It's times like this when I miss my mom even more. She would know what to say to me, but sadly she's not around. I just sit staring at the blank page. I wasn't in the mood to write. My mind was empty. I sit on the bench just looking out into the open. There's something about Jabari that I can't get out of my head. I think I'll hear him out. Every man deserves a chance. Everyone but my father should be given a second chance.

The day ends quickly, which was good considering how crappy my day started off. I made up my mind and decide I'm going to give Jabari a chance to explain himself. I leave out of class and run over to his locker, hoping to catch him before he disappears. Luckily, he was grabbing his stuff.

"Jabari?" I say a bit nervous.

"Hey, Amara." He says putting on his black leather jacket.

"I guess it isn't fair to just end things without hearing what happened. I guess I have to hear you out before I flip the switch on the electric chair." I say with my books in my hand.

"Thank you. I have to take you somewhere so I can explain. After I tell you, if you want to stay with me or leave, I will completely understand." He says with a sad look on his face. I walk with Jabari over to his car and we get in, he drives off.

As Jabari drives, he seems nervous like he had just murdered someone. He pulls over to the side of the road. He looks at me and asks me to step out of the car. Jabari gets out of the car and walks around to the back of the car and goes into the trunk pulling out a medium duffle bag. I feel like I was in a horror movie and Jabari was the killer. We walk deep into the woods. I can't tell you how many tree branches I trip over following behind him. He doesn't say much to me, and I blindly continue to follow him.

"Okay, Jabari where are we going?" I say slightly annoyed.

"We are here. Amara, listen to me. I need you to stand right here and don't move." He says nervously removing his clothes.

"Jabari, what is going on? Why are you taking off your clothes?! Are you going to tell me why you haven't returned my calls?" I yell looking at Jabari in nothing but his underwear.

"Don't be afraid, okay?" He says walking away from me.

"Jabari?!" I say inching towards him.

I couldn't believe what I saw in front of me. I fall backward onto my butt. Jabari transformed into a lion right in front of me. Jabari put his head low to the ground and slowly walks to me. There is a lion right in front of me, but it's Jabari. He's a lion, how does something like this even happen? One minute he was a perfect human teenage boy, the next he was a huge lion. I reach out and touch the lion's nose to make sure I wasn't dreaming. Once he was done being a lion, he picks up the duffle bag with his teeth and goes behind the trees to put back on his clothes. My legs become like noodles. I could barely even feel them.

I wasn't scared of him at all. I was mainly in shock more than anything. What do you say to someone who just turned into a lion right in front of you? He walks out from between the trees and weeds. Jabari sits on the ground next to me and doesn't say a word. In my head, I was trying to talk to him, but I couldn't. My brain wouldn't let my mouth move. I didn't care that he was able to change form, it was just weird. We sit in silence for an hour before I was able to find the words.

"Jabari?" I say looking down at my untied shoelaces.

"Amara, I understand if you never want to speak to me again. I just wanted you to know the truth." He says looking at me.

"No, I'm not upset with you. I mean, this is the first time that I have ever seen anyone transform into a lion." I say looking at his blank eyes.

Moments after that he drives me home, the car ride was silent. My head was up against the window. I knew that I couldn't say anything about Jabari. He was the only one I could talk to about this. We arrive at my house and just say goodbye to each other. Jabari created a massive hole in my chest, and I didn't know what to do about it. The whole thing is that now I would never be able to forget about him. The question now is, how are we going to make this work?

Guardians Of The People

It was the middle of the night the doorbell rings startling me awake. It was my dad and his friends, Michael and Jason. They were bringing him home. Jason had my dad against the wall trying to hold him up. My dad looks like he was sleeping, but he was mumbling in his sleep. He was so drunk and his mumbling so jumbled I couldn't understand anything he was saying. I should be used to him being like this, but I'm not.

"Hey Amara, he's too drunk we couldn't let him drive home. Here are his car keys." Michael says handing over the keys.

"Just lay him on the couch." I say tired and frustrated.

They both depart, leaving my drunk father to be my problem. I just look at him with utter disgust. There's not a tequila bottle in a world that's safe when he's around. I go back upstairs to my room and try to go back to sleep. I finally was about to fall back asleep, but about an hour or so later I was reawakened by my dad moving around. I get up out of my bed to make sure he wasn't trying to burn down the house. I walk down the stairs and peek around the corner. I found the person who I'm embarrassed to share the same DNA with peeing in the kitchen sink. I have never been more disgusted with someone other than him. I go back up to my room and just lay in my bed thinking of what and how many chemicals it's going to take to clean the sink. I use the sink to season chicken and wash the vegetables for God's sake.

The next morning I was so pissed at my dad. The most frustrating part is that he won't remember anything. He will never be anything other than a damn drunk. He's had a problem with alcohol my entire life, it got worse when my mom died. I remember I had to be in the fifth grade my dad picked me up from school and he had an open beer bottle half empty in the car driving me home. Even as a child I knew that was wrong. When we finally arrived back I, of course, told my mother and she was pissed, as any good parent would be. She, of course, ask why he was drinking and driving with me in the car. My dad was mad at me when she confronted him about it. His sad excuse was, "I wasn't drinking while she was in the car." Like that makes it any better. I walk over to him still sleeping on the couch and kick it. It took a few hard kicks before he started moving around.

"Hey dad! Dad!" I yell in frustration.

"Wha?" He says halfway sober as if he did nothing wrong.

"I set the bleach and gloves on the sink. You need to clean the sink. You peed in the sink last night." I say kicking the couch again.

"No, I didn't. I'm a grown man. I wouldn't do that!" He says sitting up pounding his chest.

"Well, your grown butt pissed in the sink last night! If I had my phone on me last night, you would be an Internet sensation." I say looking at him with an evil eye.

"You sound more like your mother each day." He says rubbing his eyes.

"I'm glad one of us does." I sarcastically say rolling my eyes.

My dad glances over at the clock realizing that he was going to be late to work. He jumps up trying to make himself look presentable to head to the factory. He leaves me to clean up his mess. I grab all of the cleaning supplies off the counter and proceed to the kitchen and start cleaning the sink.

I had been cleaning the sink for about 2 hours. I wanted to make sure this sink was the cleanest sink in the world. In my head, I was planning meals that weren't going to involve me having to use the sink. The doorbell ring which I guessed who was on the other side of the door. Jabari has been clingy to me since he showed me his metamorphosis. I don't blame him, being that I'm the only one besides his family that knows about him. I don't mind him always wanting to be around me. I open the door to see a dark skin man with snow-white teeth staring at me.

"Hey." Jabari gets a whiff of the bleach and puts his finger up to his nose. "Wow, you do like bleach don't you?" He giggles.

"No, just another chapter in the life of living with a drunk. My dad was so drunk last night he peed in the sink. So, bleach and acid should do the trick. Unless there some lion cleaning thing that I don't know about." I laugh letting him into the living room.

I take a break from cleaning, and head to the couch where Jabari was sitting waiting for me. I sit down by him and cuddling into his hot chest. Right now, it is the best feeling in the world. We lay on the couch and watch old bad sitcoms. It was perfect until my dad came home and walks right past me. He was heading upstairs to his room.

"He will be leaving in a minute to go and drink." I say to Jabari as I shake my head in disgust.

"Well, let's leave before he does." Jabari suggests.

We grab our things and I yell up to my dad to let him know I was leaving. Jabari decides it was time for me to meet his family. He warns me that a couple of his cousins had the gene too, and since has experienced the change. They're still getting used to it. Once he says that we arrived at his house. The last time I was here it was pitch dark, and I didn't get a good look at the house. His grandmother had the best garden I had ever seen. It looks like it was a picture right out of the magazine. There was a yellow wooden bench in the middle of the garden. The stairs looked like they needed to be fixed. Their steps were made out of concrete; the third step was falling apart. The edge of it was cracked were the banister connected to it. As soon as his car pulled up to the house his grandmother came out to greet her grandson. She used a cane to help her get around. She starts to talk to him, but I didn't understand the conversation because she was talking to him in a different language. I stand there not sure of what to do. Jabari is my first boyfriend, so meeting the family of the person you're dating is scary. Especially when you don't know what she is saying. I was wondering if she was saying something about me.

Jabari says something to her to move the attention from him to focus on me. I have never been more scared of how I looked before. I had on my favorite pair of black jeans with a beautiful white blouse. She looks at me for a minute. There is a huge knot in my throat that grew the more I didn't say anything, but suddenly I finally found my voice again.

"Hello, I'm Amara." I say nervously.

"I know who you are. My grandson talks about you all the time. It's good to meet you finally. You're a gorgeous girl." She says with a thick African accent reaching out to hug me.

"Thank you." I say.

"Grandma, did you have to tell her I talk about her all the time?" He says embarrassed.

"And dear, you can call me Minnie." She says smiling.

Walking into the house again made all the figures of lions make sense. Jabari is a lion, most of the men in his family are lions. Minnie was celebrating their heritage. Who would have thought that I would be dating a lion? Who would have thought I would be dating someone anyway? Dying with a house full of cats was my plan. Which I guess still is possible, Jabari being the cat and all. I have never had a healthy life so why should I start trying to now. Who wants to have the perfect love story? I think my story is starting off to be a little less than average, but that's okay. My happiness is all that matters.

Minnie walks with me into her home. A couple of Jabari's cousins come home from running from out of nowhere. They treated me like I was a young zebra they were about to kill, figuratively speaking of course. The youngest was his cousin, Ekon, was still trying to adjust to the change. What I have gathered from Jabari they have to be careful with their temper. They can easily kill someone if they lose control of their anger. I have to remind myself to keep Zhivago away from him. I know Jabari wouldn't hurt me, but Zhivago he will gladly destroy.

His other cousin Dajon was his second cousin on his mom's side. He was our same age and went to the same school. I had one class with Dajonn freshman year. I never would have thought he would be a lion. Honestly, who would believe that humans could change into lions? A couple of other guys came in the room but were too preoccupied with the food Minnie had cooked to worry about who I was. Jabari whispers into my ear their names. The bigger one was Shamari, and the short, skinny one was Fayden. There was a woman there in the group. She was young with a beautiful face. She could be a supermodel if she wanted. Her hair was styled in an afro that looks like a big fluffy pillow. She was tall, thick, and had a huge smile on her face. She walks right up to me and grabs me pulling me into a hug.

"Hello, I'm Bejeray. It's nice to meet you. Jabari talks about you all the time." She says.

"Nice to meet you. too" I say.

Bejeray smells like the best shea butter and herbs on the planet. It was the best scent in the world. Once she let me go, Jabari grabs my hand and pulls me over to him. There was another guy much older, and he had to be in his late twenties who came in last. He has long dreadlocks that were braided back and was incredibly buff. Fayden briefly stops eating as soon as he comes into the house, shortly after Shamari follows suit and stops stuffing his face.

"Pharaoh, come sit down, dear. Why are you acting so mysterious?" Minnie says handing over a plate of food to him.

"I apologize, grandma. Who is she?" He asks sitting at the head of the table examining the plate of food.

"She's Jabari's girlfriend. The one he's always talking about. Amara this is Pharaoh." Minnie says.

"Hi, I am Amara." I say waving at him.

"Girlfriend? Jabari I thought we talked about this? She needs to go now!" He says looking at both me and Jabari.

"Pharaoh she is okay. Let the girl stay. I want to get to know her." Minnie says coming to my defense.

"We have rules for a reason." He snarls and gets up coming toward my direction.

"I told her about them earlier this week. She knows that we all can turn into lions." Jabari says stepping in front of me.

"You told her?! Jabari you know the rule! Do you realize what can happen if she tells someone about us?" He yells.

"I wouldn't tell anyone about you guys. I know I have to keep this all a secret." I say hiding behind Jabari.

"Grandma, I told her about the legend of the Tau tribe when I first moved. I always thought the legend was a made up story until I experienced the change myself. Pharaoh, she is no threat to us." Jabari says moving close to Pharaoh.

"She's just a girl. She doesn't know anything about our people. Black Americans will never know anything about Africa or African culture." Pharaoh says going back to his seat.

"Well, it's not my fault. Last time I checked my ancestors were put in chains and beaten almost every single day, then fought for years to gain some freedom. Centuries later we are still struggling to achieve some independence. We sadly still have invisible chains on our necks. I know that my ancestors that jumped from a ship understood that death was freedom. It was better than to live a life chained up and treated worse than animals. It wasn't suicide when they decided to jump overboard they were gaining their freedom which turned into wings. They watch over us trying to help guide us." I say.

"You think you know everything." He says laughing.

"No, I don't know everything. I know that Africa is owned by every country, because of the natural resources it possesses.

Africa and African culture are constantly being whitewashed. The only difference between you and me is that your family wasn't stolen and mine were treated like black gold. Africa will never have peace as long as people see dollar signs when they look at people with melanin in their skin." I say stepping out from behind Jabari.

"Well, Black people need to learn how to respect their people before trying to venture out and learn anything about African culture. Black people are constantly putting themselves against their people. Team light skin versus team dark skin, or how about when women put chemicals in their hair to straighten it? You all need help." He says picking up a piece of bread.

"I completely agree with you. There are a lot of problems within the black community that we need to fix. For example, the issue of Black-on-Black crime. I can't tell you how many young Black boys as young as twelve know how to work a gun and sell drugs on the street before they know anything about stocks and bonds. Or the young Black girl who becomes blinded by the money he has. Not even understanding he's killing himself. She will sleep with him. He will end up making her a teenage mother, a baby will tie them together more than a ring will. Not realizing that they have just played into the hands of the colonizers. The system that was set up to make them fail." I say walking closer to the table.

"Okay, you're a smart-aleck, so let me ask you something. Why do African Americans fail at getting ahead? Why can't they seem to get it together?" He says putting the bread in his mouth.

"Black Americans have been told through the media repeatedly that our hair is nappy and that lighter skin is better. When African Americans try to break the stereotypes of wanting to try to start their own business, they're often turned away. Or when a Black person tries to go to school, it becomes hard for them to try and stay in school because their family doesn't have the money to support them. No one ever sees the real issue." I say.

"The real issue?" He asks.

"The issue starts at home. Let me give you an example of the Black home in the ghetto. There are males and a females living in the heart of the hood. The man didn't grow up with a father because his father was shot and killed. The couple created a child together, but before their child came along the man was a dope dealer. He was the breadwinner of the household, and all his woman had to do was to listen to him. He goes out every night running the streets selling to his people, knowingly killing them. He doesn't care because he needs the money. One night the man gets shot and killed because he was selling in the wrong territory. The woman is at home left to raise her five-year-old son. She can't deal with the loss of her man because he was supporting her. Now all the responsibility falls on her. Since she can't deal with the stress of it, she begins to self-medicate to cope with the loss. Crack became her new lover. That five- year- old has been watching the both his parent's making the wrong decisions his whole life. Being that's all the child knows, he will grow up to do the same thing his father did. He goes out and does the same thing that his father did, and the cycle repeats itself. Now somewhere down the line, the cycle will break because someone dared to take a chance. The pattern needs to be broken so that Black people can heal from years of pain." I say looking into Pharaoh's eyes.

"I guess you're how they say woke." He smirks.

"No, I'm an educated Black woman who was raised by a stronger Black woman. And when I am challenged, I don't back down. I jump in front of the fire. I'm just like the hundreds of Black women who have stood in the line of fire to protect their sons and daughters starring down the barrel of a gun. I'm a Black woman. I say it proudly, curly hair and all. African or African American people don't see a difference. You're still a nigger or because your African how about being called a kaffir. We both have the same struggle against racism and racist people. I may not know a lot about my ancestral background but I do know what it's like being Black in America." I say standing proud, not backing down.

"She sure told you, Pharaoh. Never seen you shut up so quickly!" Bejeray says laughing at Pharaoh.

"Well, Jabari, she might be a keeper." Pharaoh says picking up the glass of water looking at me.

I stayed at Jabari's house for a while just hanging out with his family. Minnie was dancing in the light of the fire. I sit down and watch her move effortlessly in the light. Fayden was beating on some djembe drums. Shamari was still eating. He was eating like he was on death row and he was hours away from the gas chamber. Bejeray was planting some succulents in the garden and took a break to join Minnie. Pharaoh watches me from across the fire. I think he's just waiting for me to do something so he will have a valid reason to kill me. I knew that once Jabari told me he could change into a lion, I was signing a contract that binds me for the rest of my life. I would forever have Jabari in my life because of it. This secret is something that you can't just disregard.

Jabari's grandfather shows up after a long day of work. He was very tall and almost glided when he walked. Pharaoh began to act like Fayden and Shamari did when he came through the door earlier. Minnie helped him to the chair that, until now, no one sat in. He starts talking to Minnie and he had the most profound voice I have ever heard before in my life. I swear his voice was causing the ground to shake. I assumed that Minnie started talking about me because she switched languages and he started looking at me. Jabari looks at me and tells me it's time to take me home. During the drive home, I was staring out the window until Jabari broke the awkward silence.

"So that was my family. Don't mind Pharaoh, he's just trying to feel you out. It's a lion thing. Plus, you will be happy to know that you earned his respect." He says chuckling.

"Feeling me out you say?" I say looking at him.

"Yeah, I broke a major law." He says parking in front of my house.

"The king of the jungle has laws to follow?" I say.

"Sadly, we do. We have to listen to everything Pharaoh tells us no matter what. He's sort of the leader of the tribe. We aren't supposed to tell anyone about what we can do. We are not supposed to have a girlfriend until we get control of the turning into a lion thing. Plus I don't know why he was so shocked that I told you. I think about you all the time. He shouldn't be surprised." He says.

"So what if you think about me? He wouldn't be able to know about me. He can't read your mind, or can he?" I say jokingly.

"Pharaoh can and so can the others. It's how we communicate when we change. If at the time we are going for a run and I think about you, they kind of all know about it. The month I was away from you. I couldn't stop thinking about you, it drove them crazy. Don't worry we can only read each other's mind. All your thoughts are safe." He says trying to read my blank expression.

"Oh." I say shocked. I wasn't expecting him to actually say yes to my question. This family and Jabari is getting more and more weird as I get to know them.

"Calm down, I can hear your heart beating fast. Tell me what you're thinking?" He says grabbing my hand.

"It's nothing. That has to be hard never having any privacy. So, is everyone a lion? Including Bejeray?" I say looking down at his hand.

"Yeah, but I'm used to it by now. And yes, Bejaray is the only lioness in our family. She shocked everyone when we discovered it. There have only been three other female lions. It's extremely rare. She twenty-three not that much older than Pharaoh." He says.

"I like her she seems really cool. What is the purpose of you guys? You're not hunting vampires or fairies." I say removing my focus off of our hands locked together.

"I think that God has a way of restoring balance in nature. God made our people to help be the balance of the earth. The history of our people goes back to the beginning of time. We were the first thing that God created when he decided to make the earth. What we were back then what we are now, protectors. My mother started to notice that I was experiencing signs of the change and she forced me to move down here. I was upset with her at first for making me move down here without telling me why, now I understand." Jabari pauses and places his hand on my chest. "Your heart is still beating fast. I'll let you go in so you can calm down. I don't want to give you a heart attack. Tell your heart to be still." He says moving a runaway curl from my face.

I get out of the car and walk up the stairs to the front door. I wave goodbye to him and go inside. I slid down the door and sit on the floor. I don't know what brought on the feeling of anxiety rushing through my body. I think all of the information about the Tau tribe took the strength out of me. I sit on the floor for what feels like an eternity that turned out to be only fifteen minutes. I have never felt this exhausted in my entire life than I do now. The only thing I had on my mind was a nice hot shower and my bed. Unfortunately, I made a promise to Zhivago to go to the bonfire. I quickly change into my black dress that stopped just above the knee and proceed to walk to the beach.

As I walk to the beach, I couldn't help but wonder why I haven't gotten a car yet. I can't keep walking around here in the dark. Once I finally arrive at the beach, everyone was already drunk. I sit down next to Tess who appears to be somewhat sober.

Everyone was partying and having a good time while the only thing that was on my mind was to be in my bed sleep. I tried to have some fun, but I just couldn't bring myself to do so. It's a good thing that we didn't have school in the morning. Zhivago is completely and utterly drunk. He keeps shoving beer in my face. It's not that I don't want to drink, I just don't want to become like my father. I'm trying to be better than him, not follow in his footsteps. I want to live my life trying to break the cycle. I hate that people become completely different when they drink. I stuck it out and stayed for an hour before skipping out.

I hate going to the beach because of all the sand that gets everywhere. I dealt with it and continued to walk home. I keep looking behind me trying to make sure that no one was walking up behind me. I hear the roar of an engine come up behind me. It was a white or grey pickup truck, the street lights made it look like either or. The window is rolled down and it was a young White or a Hispanic guy, who could be in his late twenties or early thirties. From the smell coming out the truck, he must be living in there.

"Hey there, young lady. Do you need a ride home?" He says with a creepy smile.

"No, I'm good. Thanks." I say hoping he would go away.

"Oh, come on, you're out here all alone." He reaches out the window and somehow grabs my hand.

"Let me go!" I yell, getting my hand free.

I run into the woods trying to get away from him. I could hear him pulling over the truck and getting out and slamming the driver door. I trip over a branch as I walk faster to get further away. He ends up catching up to me, like any typical horror story. I fight with him for a minute yelling and praying to God that someone comes and help me. He ends up picking up something and hits me over the head with it.

I fall to the ground in pain. Whatever he found to strike me with causes my brain to go haywire. My vision becomes blurry, I tried to get up and run, but I struggled to try to move. I glance over at the guy who begins to unbuckle his pants. The man climbs on top of me, with what strength I had left I use it to fight him, but it wasn't working. I was screaming so loud I hoping someone could hear me. He flips me over onto my stomach, and I try to run away. He pulls up my dress and just before he could begin to rape me, I heard the deep roar of a lion. The guy instantly takes off running. I assume the lion was Jabari and before he could get away, Jabari swiped at him with his razor-sharp claws. Once the lion comes back, he goes behind a tree and who I thought was Jabari was Pharaoh. If it weren't for his dreads, I wouldn't have been able to tell who it was.

"Amara, are you hurt? Come on stand up." He says coming to my aid.

"Pharaoh?" I say just before I pass out in his arms.

Black King

I felt like an elephant had hit me. Pharaoh was carrying me in his arms. I try my hardest to stay awake. I think I have a concussion. Pharaoh was kind of beautiful when looking at him. His name matched the way he walked and carried himself, like a king. I wasn't sure where we were. He was still carrying me through the woods. I couldn't tell if we were close to my house or his grandparent's house. I didn't know if it was him or me, but while holding me his arms, I felt like I was burning up. Once my eyes were able to focus on his face, somehow my shattered brain was able to form words.

"Pharaoh?" I say looking at his dreads.

"Amara, are you okay?" He says looking down at me.

"I think I might have a concussion. My knee hurts from when I was falling, and my right hand could be broken from repeatedly punching him in the face. Other than that I believe I'm fine." I say.

"What the hell were you doing out here! Didn't Jabari take you home?" He asks frustrated.

"He did. I was trying to be social again." I say.

"Jabari and the others are waiting for us at the house. Minnie will take a look at you. You're lucky I could smell the blood and heard you. I almost didn't make it to you." He says.

"Right, you can hear what each other is thinking."

"So now that we have gotten to know each other better, I like you. I can see that you have a lot more knowledge about history and understand how the world works. I apologize for judging you so quickly." He says looking at me.

He carried me out of the woods, and we could see the house. Everyone is standing outside waiting to come to my aid. Jabari runs and grabs me out of Pharaoh's arms. He runs me over to Minnie so she could have a look at me.

"What exactly happened to you?" Minnie says worriedly.

"Someone tried to rape her. He could have possibly been trying to kill her and sell her organs. You know how much Black organs go for? I swiped at him. I don't think he would go to the hospital. I could smell weed and alcohol on him." Pharaoh says looking at Minnie.

She examines my hand and determines that it wasn't broken. Minnie used to practice medicine in Tanzania. Jabari was a little upset. He asks Pharaoh to go out and find the guy so he can handle this himself. It's a good thing Pharaoh is alpha of the tribe and was able to calm Jabari down. Minnie left me on the couch icing my right hand. Bejeray came to look after me once Minnie walks away from me. I watch Pharaoh trying to make Jabari understand that I was okay. Minnie comes back into the living room with some potion.

"Now dear, this isn't going to taste good, but you need to drink all of this. In the morning you should feel better." She says handing over the glass.

I trusted her enough that she wasn't going to give me something that would kill me. Whatever this is was black with different herbs floating around in it. The smell alone was going to kill me. I have never in my life smelled something so putrid. I thought the smell was the worse, but the taste was awful, but I did what she instructed me to do.

"Okay, Jabari you can take her home. In the morning, you will be good as new." She says smiling.

"Thank you, Pharaoh." I say walking to the door.

"You're now one of us. So that means we are going to treat you as such." Pharaoh says cracking a smile.

"Thank you so much, Minnie." I say while Jabari helped me up from the couch.

Jabari was pissed at me. I think that he was mainly upset with Pharaoh more so than me. I really didn't pay attention to anything he had to say. In my head, I was too busy replaying what just happened to me. I owed Pharaoh my life, what could I have done if Pharaoh didn't show up and saved me? I thought I was living in hell before. I don't think I would have been able to handle the stress of being raped. He pulls up to my house and walks me directly to my door.

"Okay, do I have to chain you to the bed and make sure you stay put this time?" He says making sure I was in the house.

"No, I think I'm going to take a shower and try to get some sleep. Goodnight." I say kissing his cheek.

I close the door and look out the window, watching him drive away. I showered, washed my hair and set my hair in two strand twists. I laid in bed just thinking about what could have happened. I toss and turn trying to go to sleep. My brain was in overdrive thinking and wasn't allowing me to rest. I glance over at my desk and look at my journal. It's been awhile since I have written my feelings out.

Dear Diary:

What the hell is going on in my life? The more I try to become normal the more I lose myself. Tonight I would have been raped if Pharaoh hadn't been going out for a run. There is nothing I can do to repay him for that. I think I have learned my lesson about walking out alone that late at night. I can't keep walking around like I'm invincible. Pharaoh seems like he has a good heart. Minnie is so sweet she reminds me of my grandmother. I'm starting to believe that having a pack of lions around me is going to have its advantages.

~Amara

The Strength Of A Lion

I don't know what time my brain decided to shut down. When I woke up from my slumber, it was one in the afternoon. I examined myself to see if there was any bruising or any broken bones Minnie could have missed. I felt like I was normal, as if I wasn't attacked by a madman last night. I don't know what it was in that drink Minnie gave me, but I feel great. In my head, I keep seeing the guys face. Hopefully, the memory will go away soon.

I walk to the bathroom and examined my face, nothing. I was perfectly fine. I could hear my dad in the next room snoring. He wasn't here when Jabari dropped me off the second time. I fix myself breakfast when the doorbell rings. Of course, it was no one other than Jabari checking on me.

"So how do you feel?" He says walking through the door to the couch.

"Fine, the swelling in my hand went down. My head doesn't hurt, no bruising. What was that stuff she gave me?" I say with a confused look on my face.

"Dried kigelia fruit with a couple of other herbs. African herbs are powerful. The kings and queens of Egypt used to live off of it when they hurt themselves." He says smiling.

"Well, I feel great. African's are truly amazing." I say looking him up and down smiling.

"I want to take you out today. I asked Pharaoh to give me a few hours with you, and I'll make it up to the pack later." He says folding his hands together.

"Okay, well I need to get dressed and take down my hair, which I must warn you will take a minute, being that I have natural hair." I say leaving Jabari downstairs.

In my young life, I never thought I would be taking walks in the park with someone I love. Most of my life I have been focusing on school, I never really thought about dating anyone. Even if this thing with Jabari doesn't last, I'm happy he was the first to touch my heart. I finally get myself together and we leave going on a walk.

He could tell that something was wrong with me. I was really distant with him. I think I just had a lot of stuff on my mind. It's times like this when I miss my mom the most. She would have known what to tell me in my time of need, but I wouldn't have been able to inform her that the person I'm in love with is a lion. I don't think there is a parenting class that would have been able to help her help me with that problem.

"I can tell there is something on your mind." He says grabbing my hand.

"Pharaoh said something yesterday about me being assaulted, and my organs being stolen if he hadn't gotten there in time. What did he mean by my organs being stolen?" I look at our hands locked together.

"Okay, so you know how when we were kids, and we first learned about the history of the first president of the country, the teacher would say he had wooden teeth." He says.

"Yeah?" I say looking confused.

"He didn't have wooden teeth. Even back then people knew that when wood is wet, it swells and becomes useless. That's just plain common sense. He had the teeth of his African slave. Teeth extracted from their skulls and made into dentures. During slavery, they saw black people as creatures. Europeans had never seen anyone with dark skin before so they thought it was something wrong with them. They were examining them like they were some mythical creature. Think about it, organs are the only thing that you need to be able to live. It's not like you can go to the store and buy a kidney if you need one. Out of all the races in the world, people of African descent go missing a lot more than anyone else. What does all of that tell you?" He says slowing down his pace.

"The world is so dangerous that you can be murdered for having the same blood type as someone wealthy?" I say slowing my pace to match his.

My phone starts to go off. It was my father texting me asking where I was. I ignored it and put my phone back into my pocket. I just didn't feel like dealing with him today or any other day for that matter. It's time for me to move on. The only reason

I'm staying around is to finish school. My mother left me enough money I can get a place out of town. What's the point of waiting around? All we do is argue when he's not drunk. I shouldn't be suffering along with him. Even when my mom was here, he still wasn't around much. Now more than ever we are distant from each other.

"Amara, I have a question for you." He pauses.

"Okay ask." Pausing for his question.

"Can I meet your dad?" He says waiting for a response.

"No, absolutely not." I say letting go of his hand.

"Why?" He asks.

"My dad has damaged me to the point of no return. I'm used to him being in and out of my life. For most of my life, he has preferred to be with his friends more than me. I was 5 years old, and I told my mother that he loved his friends more than me. The only thing he has given me is digital affection." I say with my arms folded.

"I understand." He says.

"No, I don't think you do. He would come home late during the week. He would just go to bed. I don't know at what point I started hating him, but over the years it has gotten worse. He didn't have his father in his life, so he doesn't know how to love. I'm a woman, so it affects me more than him. You know the old saying, *a woman will fall in love with a man who resembles her father?*" I say in a calm voice.

"I have heard it." He says.

"Well, I'm not. I'm looking for anything but him. I don't know how my mother put up with it for so long. Maybe it's an effect of slavery. In slavery, so many families were separated that you had to find the strength not to love anyone. My mother was the head of the household not my dad. He can barely take care of himself. I'm trying my hardest not to fit into a stereotype. The media keeps us at the bottom, without an option to get to the top. A stereotype of Black people." I pause taking a seat on the bench.

"Amara, you cannot keep walking around thinking that the reason he wasn't there is your fault. Some people are not meant to be fathers, he's one of them. You are not a stereotype, you're anything but. You are hurting, and you have been for far too long. It will take some time before you can start healing." He sits down next to me lifting my head up with his pointer finger.

"Some men need to see through a woman eyes. Then I believe only then they will understand. Men can become emotionless when they're hurting. They make the people around them hurt along with them." I say.

We sit in silence on the bench for a while. It's hard to start a conversation up after you have discussed your issues about your father. My brain was spinning out of control with ways to start up a conversation with him again. Most of the time I try to live my life knowing that our relationship will never be good. It will forever be broken. At some point, you just get tired of waiting for daddy to come home.

"The reason I don't want you to meet him is that I don't plan to talk to him ever again once I graduate. My mother did everything and then some. My father wasn't responsible at all. He never paid his bills on time. My mother gave him a couple of bills, and he wouldn't pay those on time. I can't tell you how many times the lights have been turned off and she had to pay it. The only reason my mother stayed with him I believe is that she wanted to give me a healthy family life, but she wasn't happy. Her death, even though a painful one, gave her freedom from him." I say.

"I don't want to upset you, but if I can ask, what was your breaking point?" He asks stumbling over his words.

"My dad had surgery on his back. The morning of his surgery he wanted my mother to drive his car instead of hers, so she did. We waited for hours for him to get out of the operation. When he was out the doctor gave him a prescription, and he didn't even have the money for his medication. He had his friend's credit card. Any way to make a long story not so long, we went to go pick up his prescription, and my nose was running so I looked for a tissue. I looked into the center console and found condoms. My mother had a hysterectomy when I was in sixth grade. My father had a vasectomy when I was young. What would a man who was snipped as well as his wife need condoms for? I was done with him when I found them." I say looking at Jabari in the eyes.

"Amara, I'm sorry." He says.

"Me too, so do you want to get something to eat? I know you have to get back to your family soon." I say in a happy tone changing the subject.

We get up and walk back to the car. I don't possess any lion powers, but I could tell that Jabari felt terrible for asking me about my sad life. He had his arm resting on the center console I grab it and lock fingers with him. He glances over and smiles at me.

The one thing I like about Jabari is that he seems to listen to me. It makes me feel like he understands even though he doesn't. No one will understand or have to deal with my pain other than me. I have become the agony of a thousand slaves for far too long - invisible scars that will never heal.

Black Queen

I need a vacation from school, every teacher has been stuffing college down my throat. I know that college is critical, but right now I don't know what I would be going for. It would be a waste of money for me to go. My brain hurts from having to write so many essays. I have the highest scores possible, so that's not a problem. I have no motivation to attend. I can't seem to be focused on what I need to do.

It's been a while since I have visited my mom's grave. It could be why I haven't been myself, her way of reminding me to come to see her I guess. I miss seeing her button nose and high cheekbones. Her skin was the shade of mocha, and she had long wavy black hair. She always gave the best hugs. I was so zoned out I walked right into Zhivago and Tess. We dropped all of our books. When I realize what happened it instantly snapped me out of my head.

We all struggle for a moment trying to sort through all the school books, trying to figure out what belonged to who. Tess was in a good mood as always. Zhivago was a little too touchy-feely with me. I don't like to hurt people's feelings, but I think I have to with Zhivago. I don't think he realizes that I'm with Jabari. If Jabari saw how he was touching me, I think he wouldn't be able to control the lion in him. I pick up my last book and apologize to everyone, but of course, Zhivago had to start running his mouth. Lately, he has been finding any excuse to talk to me. He's starting to get a little bit pushy. What makes things worse is the fall dance is coming up, and everyone is trying to find dates to the dance.

"So, Amara are you going to the dance?" He says happily waiting for my response.

"I don't know yet. I haven't talked to Jabari about it yet." I say hoping to end the conversation.

"Jabari, huh?" He says not amused.

"Yeah." I respond.

"Is he even here today? He's been missing a lot of school lately." He says.

"He's here actually. I should see him at lunch later." I say looking for a way to get out if this conversation.

"Amara, I want to go to the dance with you!" He says grabbing my hand.

"Zhivago, I'm with Jabari you know that." I say.

Just when this moment couldn't get any worse than it possibly could have gotten, it did. Zhivago is acting like a little kid. I only see him as my brother and nothing else. He doesn't even know Jabari. Ever since Jabari got here, he hasn't liked him. I don't understand males sometimes. Jabari came out of nowhere and join in on the conversation.

"Hey, beautiful, how are you?" Jabari says kissing my forehead.

"I'm fine." I say wishing he hadn't kissed me.

"Hey, Zhivago." He says calmly.

"What's your deal? Disappearing for a month, breaking Amara's heart." He says pulling me away from Jabari.

"He had a good reason that's not for you to be worried about." I say pushing him away from me.

"Zhivago, if you like having your hands I suggest you never grab Amara like that again." He says pulling me back.

This was the first time I have felt like a dogs chew toy. I tried my hardest to break this up before it got way out of hand, but sadly it was too late. While Jabari pulled me toward him, Zhivago punches him in his face. The amount of fear I had in my stomach was unbearable. The last thing Jabari needed was for everyone to know his secret. I have only seen him change once. I couldn't tell if it was because he was notably mad but he was shaking so hard, I just knew he was about to change. Zhivago jumped back not sure what was happening. I knew Jabari was struggling trying to fight the lion part of himself. I took a chance and jumped in front of him. At this point, I didn't know how much of himself was still human and could understand me.

"Jabari calm down. Look at me, I'm okay. It's okay, breath." I say placing my hands on his face trying to get his focus off of Zhivago.

He slowly stopped shaking. His breathing starts to not feel so tense and hard. By the time he calmed down Principal Madison had shown up as mad as could be. She took Jabari and Zhivago to her office. The only thing I could think of was Jabari losing it in the office.

The entire time in English I could hardly even focus on anything Ms. Angel was saying. Everything she was saying was going in one ear and out the other. The only thing I had on my mind was Jabari. I stare at the clock for most of the class praying that class would end quickly. I glance down at my phone hoping that he would text me and let me know that everything was fine. When the bell finally rings I run out of class to the principal's office. When I finally got to the office no one was there. I made my way to Zhivago's locker he wasn't there. I text Jabari to see where he was but he never responds.

Lunchtime comes around and everyone is just looking at me like I was a freak. Tess and Jonny were all into each other but broke away once I walked over to the table. Eric was looking for the answer to a quiz online. Anne was working on her project for English. Chris was stealing food from Anne when she wasn't looking. When I reached the table, everyone stops what they were doing to focus on me.

"Amara, what the hell happened?" Tess says leaning on Jonny.

"Yeah, Jabari looked like he was going to explode." Anne says.

"Zhivago was out of line. Jabari was just pissed that's all. Did any of you hear anything?" I query.

"Zhivago is suspended for two weeks. Jabari got in school suspension." Anne says.

"Okay." I say relieved.

After school, I waited by Jabari's car for him. I was nervous not knowing how he would feel. It's been over three months since he's been a lion. I know he's used to changing, but he could have killed Zhivago today without question. I scanned everyone trying to find him. I start playing a stupid game on my phone when he appeared right in front of me. He still looks upset, and I don't blame him.

"Hey, are you okay?" I say knowing the answer.

"Let's go!" He says not looking at me.

I could tell by the tone of his voice that he didn't want to talk about anything. I took my journal out of my bag and start drawing. A part of me wishes he was still human. I feel like he's suffering and just not showing it. The one thing about Black men is that they are told that they can't express their feelings. I finally notice that he was taking me home and I didn't want to go home. I wanted to be with him to help him.

"Jabari, I don't want to go home. I can go to your grandmother's house." I say looking at him.

"No, I'm dropping you off at your house. I want to be alone right now." He says through his clenched teeth.

"No! Right now you don't need to be alone." I say looking confused.

"Amara! I'm dropping you off, and that is it!" He yells causing me to jump.

"Okay, you don't need to yell at me. I was trying to make sure you were okay." I say getting out the car.

I slam the car door and rush to get into the house. I was pissed. I'm the only one outside of his family that knows about him. At this present time, I didn't know if it was Jabari or the lion I was talking to. I thought I was going to be able to relax for a change, but I could not. My dad hasn't been drinking yet, so he has a bright mind.

"Who was that dropping you off? You better not have a boyfriend you're too young for that!" He yells trying to get up off the couch.

"It's none of your concern of who brings me home, and I'm eighteen years old! I can be with whoever I choose!" I yell walking up the stairs.

"You're my daughter! It is my business." He roars.

"That only because you're not drunk right now because you're suffering, I suffer too!" I shout.

"I have done all that I can do as a dad. What should be important is the love I have for you. You should never forget that." He stands up.

"Yeah it should, but I will never forget the beer bottle in your hand as you sit on the bar stool with your friends. Have fun drinking yourself to death tonight. Goodnight." I say turning around facing him.

He says nothing back. So I stomp upstairs to my room, closing and locking the door behind me. I slide to the floor and sit there, exhausted from life. I have cried so many tears I could water Africa for a hundred years. I hope my kids don't have to deal with this type of stress in the future. At what point does someone just go insane form this type of pain. I think everyone is crazy, or maybe I'm just the one that's sick. Sometimes death is better than living, life can be worth living just not mine.

Dear Diary:

Just a really fucked up day.

~Amara

I stay locked away in my room for the rest of the night. I just lay in my bed not knowing what to do with my life. My phone keeps ringing off the hook. It was Jabari trying to talk to me. I was pretty sure he wanted to explain why he just went off earlier. I'm not in the mood for talking to anyone right now. I just want to try to make my pain go away. I don't think that will ever happen. Not as long as I'm in this hell hole of a house.

I was getting ready to go to bed, but sadly someone was ringing my doorbell and would not go away. I was so drained from the day I barely had the energy to walk down the stairs. I was hoping that it would be someone to take me away, but no it was anything but.

"Pharaoh?" I say confused as I look out the window of the front door.

"We need to talk. Can I come in?" He says loudly behind the door.

I let him in the house offering him a seat and something to drink. He just sits at the end of the couch waiting for me to have a seat myself.

"Jabari told me what happened earlier, or more like I read his thoughts. Amara you having knowledge of us comes with great responsibility. I know it wasn't your fault, but we can't let that happen again. If he would have changed forms, I don't even know what would have happened." He says folding his hands.

"I know, luckily he was able to stop himself." I say.

"I know, but that's not the reason I came over here. I came to give you a little history lesson. Ancient Egypt, our ancestors, valued lions. Every tomb, any artifact has some sort of feline on it. Look at the Sphinx of Giza - the face of an African man but the body of a lion. Why do you think they did that?" He asks.

"The lion symbolizes power and strength." I say trying to come up with a better answer.

"Yes, that's one reason. African's of that time also chose it because a lion's job is to protect its people. When it's threatened or its family is threaten, a lion doesn't think it attacks without question. Lions are the only animal that can walk through the land of Africa and have nothing to fear. The Egyptian chose the lion because a lion doesn't bow down to anyone. We are descendants of kings and queens and should walk as such." He says with his voice thicker than usual.

I sit back analyzing everything Pharaoh is saying to me. I'm learning a lot about my history through Jabari and his family. I think that Pharaoh was telling me this history to read between the lines. Though what he was saying to me was simple it was also very complicated.

"Wow, that was incredibly beautiful." I say not knowing what to say.

Pharaoh gets up and walks to the door. I can never get over how massive he was. Most of the men in town are old, but even the young ones are not in shape like Pharaoh is. He was walking down the stairs when she stops and turns around.

"Amara, if you have any doubt about Jabari don't. He praises the very ground you walk on." He says getting in the car and driving away.

"My life just got a lot more complicated than what it needs to be." I say talking to the presence of Pharaoh left in the wind.

I don't remember exactly when I finally fell asleep, but I did. I woke up feeling more exhausted than ever. I didn't have the energy to dress nice today. I wore an old pair of black yoga pants with an oversized sweatshirt with a cat on it. I walk downstairs past my dad and left for school. It was a beautiful day out considering I felt utterly crappy. Usually, this walk is very short, but today it felt long. It's like I was walking uphill never reaching the top.

My friends seemed pretty happy, but I wasn't. It was early enough that no one was in class yet which was giving me the perfect opportunity to sleep. I put my head down and wrapped my arms around my head, blocking out the light. I was able to get a bit of a power nap before a loud noise of textbooks slamming on the desk woke me up.

"What is the deal?" I yell.

"Good morning." He smiles.

"Jabari?!" I say semi-upset.

"I wanted to apologize for my behavior yesterday. This weekend the library is having a spoken word event. I would like for you to go with me." He says happily.

"Jabari, after yesterday I'm completely exhausted." I say.

"I know, but please let me make it up to you." He says grabbing my hand to kiss.

"Okay, I'll go. Now get to the dean's office before you really get suspended." I say giving in.

Just as quick as I could snap my finger it was the weekend. I was dressed in a burgundy shirt with black pants. I debated for a while about shoes and decided to go with chunky heels. I was in a good mood, so I decided to do my makeup.

Jabari came to my door dressed in all black. I think he was lying when he told me he couldn't read my mind. We matched perfectly. He walks me to the car opening the door. I know he's trying to be a gentleman, but still, I can open the door.

The drive to the library wasn't that long. It was a block or two away from school. The library was a packed house. I used to come here every day when I would be waiting for my mom to get home from the doctors. I have never seen it this packed before. Luckily, we were able to find good seats.

Performer after performer, all the poems were powerful and spoke volumes. I sat waiting for the next performer when the host called my name. Instantly the blood left my body.

"Jabari, why would you sign me up?" I question him furiously.

"You're always writing. You will be fine." He says smiling.

"Is Amara here?" The host asks.

"She's right here." Jabari says raising my hand.

"When this is over I will show you fear even a lion will not be able to handle." I say grunting through my teeth.

I walk up to the stage pissed at Jabari. I grab the mic clueless as to what to say. He must have read over my shoulder and saw a poem I was writing. Jabari had no right to put me in a position I won't be able to back out of.

"Hello this is my first time doing spoken word, so I apologize if I suck." I swallow the spit in my mouth and look at my notebook. I take a deep breath and go for it.

"I have the blood of a thousand slaves rushing through my veins. My ancestors jumped from ships falling to their death. The sea became their casket. Water filling their lungs as they took their last breaths - bringing a whole new meaning to bloody water. Families lost never to become whole again. They were hung from trees like the sweetest fruits anyone has ever had. Slavery ended 400 hundred years ago, and people believe there's no such thing as racism. No such thing as racism? How about the hundreds of Black men with gunshots in their chests? Mothers crying as their babies' blood paints the street red. Or how about when Hispanics are told to speak English. How about the countless of Muslim girls who have had their hijabs ripped from their heads. News flash, slavery ended 265 years ago, segregation 99 years ago, we have only had freedom for 50 years, and we still are in shackles." I say with a fire I have never had before.

As I step off of the stage and walk back to my seat, I realize everyone was cheering me on. I was feeling eerie getting up in front of a whole crowd of people, but then a sense of euphoria washes over me. Once I reach my seat, Jabari was the loudest one clapping. I thought of myself as a tree. I'm growing and spreading my roots deep into the earth. Even a tree breaks under pressure sometimes. I was hoping I wasn't going to crack on stage. After the event reality set in we were happy. It wasn't until Jabari pulls into my driveway. The mood in the car changed completely once we were sitting staring at my old broken down house. The garden that my mother grew flowers in was completely dead. The house just needed to be destroyed and rebuilt. The bricks have even started to crack.

"Amara…" Jabari says grabbing my hand.

"Yes." I say looking at my hand interlocked with his.

"I can sense that you're trying to force yourself to love someone." He says with a soft tone.

"You would be right. Love is able to make you both calm and nervous at the same time. It's sometimes the only reason why you can wake up in the morning. Looking into the eyes of someone you love and knowing they love you back is the best thing you can ever experience. I'm struggling to get to that point." I say trying not to hurt his heart.

"I can't promise anything, but I will try not to let you down." He says.

"Since you bring up history all the time. Our ancestors lost their loved ones. The ones who they decided to make two hearts with and become one with. Trapped, beaten by their masters, and broken down to think of themselves as nothing. I'm a slave to my own pain. I'm trying not to wait for my master to give me my freedom papers. I will take my freedom when I'm ready." I say leaning in to kiss him.

My life can never have peace in it. I thought my dad was gone out drinking for the night. He being gone is something I can always depend on. The entire time I was making out with Jabari, he was looking at us out the window. We were too busy with each other to notice him storming out of the house. My dad grabs Jabari out of the car. My dad just started fighting Jabari for no reason. I jump out trying to pull my dad off of him. He quickly turned to me. Jabari didn't even lift a finger, he had better control of himself this time around. Soon my dad tired himself out just enough to stop. The rage he had for Jabari soon transferred to me. He gets up off the ground and slaps me knocking me to the ground.

"You stay away from my daughter! I know what all you young guys want to do with girls. Amara will not be one of those girls!" He says looking at Jabari.

Jabari just looks at my dad wanting to kill him, and I don't blame him. The problem with my dad is that he is so unpredictable. My dad grabs me by my hair dragging me into the house, without even giving me the chance to stand up. He slams the door while throwing me onto the couch.

"You better not see that boy anymore!" He yells.

"His name is Jabari!" I scream.

"I don't give a damn what his name is. I better not catch you with him anymore." He roars at me.

I get up from the couch and start to head up to lock myself in my room. He grabs me by my hair again, pulling me off the stairs and back down to the floor.

"What is the matter with you?" I scream getting up from the floor again.

"I will not have a hoe for a daughter!" He shouts.

"I'm not a hoe, and he is my first boyfriend."

"You still a virgin?" He questions with his hand on his side.

"Yes, and if I wasn't, it's none of your business." I shriek disgusted with him.

"I'm your father. It is my damn business!" He screams in frustration.

"That title is earned not given." I holler stomping my feet.

"Watch your mouth!" He says pointing his finger at me.

"Go to hell, Terrence!" I yell.

He pulled my grandmothers old leather belt that she never wore. It's only purpose was to give out whippings. This belt is ancient but looks brand new. When my grandmother whipped me with for the first time I had never felt pain like that ever before. I think this belt was used to beat the slaves. My dad was standing in front of the stairs, he turns to lock the door with the key. After he secures the door, he runs over to me swinging the belt hitting me in my face. I don't even know how many hits of the belt I took before he starts punching me. He keep switching between his fist and the belt. I didn't know how long the ass whooping lasted, but it was long enough.

"I'm finished with you get out of my sight." He says out of breath.

"I hate you!" I say running to my room.

Paw

I lock myself in my room. I was so severely hurt I could barely move without a single part of me not hurting. Luckily each of the bedrooms has a bathroom. I ran the hottest bath water ever. My face was bruised from my dad punching me. There was massive welt on my face from the belt striking me in the face. Once I remove my clothes, I could see more welts starting to rise up. I took pictures of myself documenting everything. I have been disciplined before, but this was different, this was rage. If there were anything positive to come out of this, I would have the best sleep of my life tonight.

I look out of the window and make sure that my father was gone before I left out of my room. The welts were going down, slowly but they still were obvious. I want to sleep the day away, but Jabari wasn't going to let me. I heard the engine of his car outside of my house. I quickly change out of my shorts and put on some pant and opens the door. Visibly he was fine no bruises or anything. He looks like no one even touched him.

"Amara?! What did he do to you?" He asks turning my head to get a better look at the welt, which was still sore.

"He beat my ass." I say frowning at the pain.

"This was a beating? What type of man would do this to a woman? Even if you are his daughter, this isn't right." He says.

Jabari usually doesn't speak with an African accent, but when he is upset, it comes out. I went into the kitchen grabbing an ice pack for my face. Jabari follows me upset that I was hurt. I was too embarrassed to look at him. I was walking back into the living room when he stops me, forcing me to look at him.

"Jabari, you should go before he shows up. Then there will be round two." I say looking at him.

"Amara?" He says.

"The slaves were beaten, why?" I say putting the ice pack on my face.

"What does this have to do with slavery?" He asks.

"The slaves were beaten to show them obedience. It was used to correct the actions that the master found wrong. Once slavery ended, and they were no longer slaves you think the beatings stopped then? No, the slaves were so afraid of being prisoner they made sure that they did nothing wrong to anyone. Their children had to be taught discipline. If their child even looked at a person of the opposite race wrong, a slap on the hand was used to correct the wrong. Under the most severe situations, shoes were used on their butts." I say walking over to the freezer.

"I'm not following." He says raising an eyebrow.

"They would discipline their children this way because their mothers didn't want their child with a rope around their necks. This way of thinking was passed down from generation to generation. There isn't a black child alive that hasn't been raised of the slave way of thinking." I say.

Jabari runs and gives me a hug but was careful not to squeeze too hard. I kiss his cheek wanting him to leave before my dad came home. He soon let me go giving me one kiss on the lips. Black love can be powerful when you least expect it to be.

"Every time I look at you, I see all the love of Africa, but I also see the pain that keeps holding it back." He says walking to the door.

If there's one thing, I will be able to take with me in old age. A woman heart is sacred. It's more valuable than gold. A woman will only give all of herself to someone she loves. A man gives his heart only to the one he loves. He may be with other women, but he saves his heart for the one he loves. It's his gift to his woman. He will never waste his love.

I slept for the rest of the day after Jabari left. We have school tomorrow, and I would like to be in a lot less pain. Each time I turn over in my bed I was in intense pain. I don't think he hit me hard enough to break a rib. I was going to go back to sleep when I remembered my mom's heavy painkillers. My mother's hospital bag was still sitting in the basement collecting dust.

Every single step I took hurt walking down the stairs into the basement. I reach the bottom of the steps. My mother's black bag looked grey because of all the dust. A couple of months ago I didn't have the strength to go through it. Whatever strength I had left that wasn't beaten out of me last night was it. I unzip her bag. All of her clothes smelled just like her. I reached the bottom of her the bag and found her painkillers. Also at the bottom of the bed along with the medication was a letter addressed to me. I placed everything neatly back into the bag and headed upstairs.

I sit on the floor not knowing what's inside the letter. My hands started to shake so bad. My stomach was in the most prominent knot ever. There was a burning pain in my throat. I haven't even read anything yet, and tears started to fill my eyes. I slowly opened the handwritten letter.

My Dearest Amara,

If you're reading this, then it means I didn't make it. If I did beat this disease, put this letter back and get out of my stuff.

I love you more than my own life. There's nothing I would not do for you. You gave me a reason for living. If I didn't have you in my life, I wouldn't be the woman I am. I know that me leaving you is hard. It was harder for me to leave you.

If I could give you some last-minute advice. A mother's love runs so deep. I know that you don't understand that yet. Mothers are the most dangerous thing on this planet. A mother will do anything to protect her child. She will risk it all without hesitation. Amara, even in death I will still be your protector -even when you think I'm not around, I'm there right there by your side.

Amara, I will always be with you. Death will never split us. I love you, my little piece of heaven.

Love,

Mom

I feel like the letter although bittersweet confirms her death. I will never get this type of love ever again. I haven't cried this hard since I saw her slip away from me. I feel like I lost her all over again. This pain I feel will never go away.

I'm so lucky that the welt on my face went down just in time for Monday. I still had bruises and marks everywhere else, but those were easy to hide from everyone. Jabari texted me letting me know he would be taking me to school like normal. He parked at the end of the street. I hop in his car, and he always smiles when he sees me. After the hell I went through over the weekend, I'm praying that I can have a semi-normal week.

"You look a lot better. How are you?" He says pulling off.

"I feel like I'm slowly dying of old age." I say looking out the window.

"You're welcome to come home with me after school if you would like. Or are you super eager to go home after school? Plus, Bejeray really wants to see you again." He says laughing.

"I think that you know damn well I don't want to go home." I say laughing at him.

I went through the day at school acting like a reasonable human being. I met up with Jabari as usual. I was happy I got to see Minnie again. It's been a couple of weeks since I have seen her. According to Jabari, she has been asking about me. It's nice to know that at least someone around here has a healthy life, besides the whole changing thing.

"Okay, before we arrive at the house there's been a couple of changes. We have a new member to join us." He says gripping the steering wheel.

"Okay." I say not sure of what else to say.

"His name is Sir." He says laughing.

"What? Sir? S-I-R?" I ask surprised.

"Yeah, I know. His mother, my aunt, says the reason she named him Sir was because when people address her son they will address him as Sir." He says laughing.

"Okay." I chuckle.

"I'm no one to judge, people barely know how to say my name." I say.

"Oh, and by the way, he's sort of taking the whole morphing into a lion thing to his head." He warns.

As soon as we arrive at Minnie's house, everyone comes rushing out of the house. Minnie was smiling happily to see me. All the boys came out of the house. Fayden runs over to me hugging me so tight. Shamari wasn't home from school yet. Dajon, who was the tallest of everyone in the house, hasn't been there. He was pulled from school. Minnie's fear is that he is going to hurt someone because he has been so aggressive lately.

"Amara, where have you been?" Fayden says happily.

"Hey, Fayden, I have been around. You're looking good." I say.

"Thanks, I have been doing a lot more running. I'm starting to put on weight." He laughs.

"How's school coming along?" Dajon asks.

"It's going great." I answer.

"Amara, I'm so happy to see you again! You have to come over here more often." Bejeray comes running out of the house exclaiming.

There's just something about being over here that makes me feel normal. I hang out with Minnie for a while before Jabari wants to take me away. He wants to go on a run with me, I climb on to

Jabari who was now a lion, and he takes off. I have never experienced this type of speed before in my life. He was running at top speed and going faster by the second. The trees look blurry.

I was having so much fun. This was a change from the last couple of weeks. Lately, I have been feeling like I'm never going to get out of this shit hole of a life. It's nice to have a break from life, even if it's just for a couple of hours. Sometimes I feel like eating glass is better than being at home. I hop off of Jabari's back. I look into his eyes and was not even scared that he would hurt me. He stays in his lion form, and I walk beside him. It was nice just having someone to listen to you as you vent. Even though he couldn't talk back, it was still lovely.

"Jabari, if it's possible I would like to hear you roar." I ask stepping in front of him.

He tilts his head to the side and stops walking. It's almost like he was debating whether or not he should do it. He took a deep breath and then realized a massive roar. I cover my ears to try and stop them from ringing. The sleeping birds above us in the tree flew away. I couldn't help but smile, it was awesome. It took about five minutes before the others found us in the woods. If it weren't for their manes I wouldn't be able to tell anyone apart. Pharaoh was the biggest out of all of them. His mane was a golden color. Fayden's was just starting to grow in, and it looks like it was going to be a light brown color. Dajon's mane was a deep dark brown color. Jabari had a different mixture of browns and yellow. It just all depends on the lighting. Bejeray was the easiest to spot out of them all. She was the only female, so no mane. They all circled around us. They pause, and all start to roar at the same time. I think after today I'm going to need a hearing aid.

After we arrive back at the house, I wait for Jabari to change and take me home. Jabari's grandfather was sitting in the kitchen eating. I was really nervous about meeting him. I took a seat at the table and introduced myself. He was wearing a black baseball hat, with some weird cross on it. His brown button-up looks like it was ancient. The pocket over his heart was slightly torn at the bottom. As soon as I grab the chair I notice he was staring me down.

"Hello, I'm sorry I didn't get to introduce myself the last I was here. I'm Amara." I say.

"I know. I'm very familiar with you. Jabari and my wife talk about you all the time." He says examining every part of me.

"Okay, I know the last time I was here I had to leave." I say before he cut me off from finishing my sentence.

"Look, I'm going to stop you right here. I don't trust you. Whatever my grandson sees in you is fine, but I think you're just here for the thrill. In the moment of pressure, you will crack and put us all at risk." He says waving the knife he was using to cut his food.

"I'm sorry that you feel that way. I can assure you that I'm not a threat to your family." I say getting up from the table and proceed to go outside.

I sit on the bench outside and feel uncomfortable. Pharaoh felt the same way about me at first. He eventually came around. I'm the only person outside of his family that knows about them. I don't blame him for being on the defensive about me. I watch

Bejeray doing flips in the yard. She so light on her feet it's unbelievable. Jabari comes out and finds me somewhat smiling, but I think his instincts could tell that something was wrong. He drives me halfway home. He pulls over midway, and I walk the rest of the rest of the way home. I'm just starting to heal from the last beating I received, don't want another one so soon, so we take precaution.

I, like every other teenager, I can't find peace when going home. My father was sadly home when I walk up to my house. I put the key in the door, turning it and instantly regretting it. I was hoping that he would be passed out sleep on the couch, but I can never be so lucky. Drug and alcohol abuse affects the Black community the most. Why is that? Is it because we are kept at the bottom without a chance of being able to get ahead? Or because of the amount of stress we are under? I think more Black people need to take mental health seriously. There's so much pain that will never be healed if it's not addressed. I try sneaking past him hoping that the football game would keep him distracted enough.

"Amara, Don't act like you don't see me. Come here we need to talk." He says.

"Shit." I mumble to myself walking to the couch.

"So how have you been?" He says looking at me.

"Fine." I say.

"How's school?" He says turning down the TV.

"Fine." I say staring at the TV.

"Is that the only word you know?" He growls.

"No." I say trying not to make eye contact with him.

"You and I have to figure out how to work things out. I'm still your daddy whether you like it or not. I know you and I are going through something. You have one more time to disrespect me like that. Amara, you need to control your smart ass mouth." He says.

I nod and get up from the couch trying to go to my room. He grabs my hand, which was balled up into a fist. I look down at him. He says nothing just looking at me.

Suddenly a power rises up in me. Maybe it was the spirit of my mother. "I have given you the respect of still calling you my dad, but I must remind you that I'm eighteen. Under the law, I'm a legal adult. If you beat me like that again, I will press assault charges on you. Then you will have to wake up in a cell every day knowing that I will never come see you. You will also know that I'm the one who put you in that whole. I suggest you never do that again. I have made several digital copies documenting what you did. I also have a couple of printouts. Don't try looking for them either. You will never find them. Let me go!" I say looking him directly into his eyes.

A part of me liked seeing the fear in his eye. A man that really isn't a man turns back into a boy. The one thing about me is that I know how to cut the head off of a venomous snake without being bitten. When it comes to my father, regardless of whatever he feels he needs to understand I will take him down without question. I'll give him his respect, but only if he plays by my rules.

It's late at night, and I was just about finished my homework before Jabari calls wanting to talk.

"Hey, Jabari." I say.

"Good evening, my love." He says.

"So what do I owe the pleasure of your call?" I get up and move to my bedroom window.

"Well, the king of the jungle just wants to check on his love." He says laughing

"I'm fine thanks for asking. And lions aren't the king of the jungle." I laugh loudly.

"What do you mean the lion isn't the king of the jungle?" He says puzzled.

"I'm pretty sure I know your answer but who do you think is the king of the jungle the lion or the elephant?" I say looking out the window.

"The lion of course. There shall be no other." He says.

"Okay, the elephant is the true king. Although it doesn't have as many kills as a pack of lions, it has the biggest heart. Both animals are protectors, but when their fellow elephant dies, they cry." I say.

"Elephant kill more humans than lions." He says.

"True, but elephants shake the ground in a way lions can't." I say.

"You know your one smart woman." He says chuckling.

"Thanks, well I have homework to finish. I'll see you tomorrow." I laugh.

"Goodnight my love." He says.

AISHA BUFORD-MORRISON

Black Love Equals Power

I carry the heart of Africa in my hand

I look up and see a man who doesn't know me

He considers the heart to be gold

The man snatches ripping the heart right out of my hands

He abuses it

Stripping it of its gold, diamonds, and oil

The heart weakens slowly cracking turning into dust

A once strong heart was now left sick

Disease spreads through it killing it slowly

The heart becomes cold in the hands of its perpetrators

The heart of Africa will beat again

Only when it returns home

The park has become my little escape from home. I set up a blanket for me to sit on and doodle. I don't know what I enjoy more writing or drawing. Writing poetry gives me a chance to play around with words, plus I seem to do that more. For me drawing feels more structured, although I'm a decent drawer. No matter what, the art will always speak louder than the artist. The only reason I have been drawing a lot more is that we have an important art project that is due. We have to present it to the entire school for extra credit. I don't need it, but a couple of extra points couldn't hurt. I still have no idea what I'm going to draw. The topic is love. I have no idea what love is. The only love I have ever experienced is unconditional love from family. I never have had the chance to earn someone's love. I believe that conditional love is more real than unconditional love from family because you never did anything to earn it.

I had headphones in and didn't hear Jabari coming up behind me. He startles me a bit, causing me to jump. I should be more careful about being in the park by myself. I wasn't even supposed to see him today. How did he find me?

"Did anyone ever tell you not to sneak up behind people? I was about to take one of your nine lives. How did you even know I was here?" I laugh.

"I can smell you. I can easily sniff you out of an entire crowd without even trying." He says kissing me on the cheek.

"I forget you're a lion sometimes." I turn to look at him.

"Plus, you had headphones on and couldn't hear me calling you. From the looks of it, you're drawing. I think you missed me." He grabs the sketchbook out of my hands.

I was drawing a lion, trying to get an idea of what to do for my art project. He examined the lion, I guess he thought I was drawing him. Which maybe I was subconsciously thinking of him. I waited for him to say something to me.

"Well, are you going to say something about it?" I ask.

"It's beautiful, Amara." He says.

"You can have it if you want it." I say smiling.

"Are you sure? Thank you! Well, I would love for the artist to sign it for me." He says making a face.

He handed my sketchbook back to me. I signed my first name with a heart and was careful not to tear it. We just sat in the park and just talk about nothing. Turns out when they start transitioning, according to Jabari, it's almost similar to going through puberty but worse. They have constant mood swings, eating habits began to change. I have only ever seen him eat meat, not many vegetables. Most of the time he wants to bite everyone's head off. His mother was worried about him because she knew what was going to become of him. He misses her I do know that.

"Jabari, can I ask you something?" I say.

"Sure." He says playing with my hair.

"What does love mean to you?" I say watching his fingers mess with my curls.

"Love is the best thing in the world for someone to experience. Looking into the eyes of someone you love and knowing they love you back is the best thing you can ever experience. One day I see myself marrying the one who has my heart. Having a child." He says focusing on each part of my face.

"Oh." I say not knowing what to say.

"What about you?" He says.

"Well considering how I'm a Black woman and have a higher chance of dying of a pulmonary embolism after childbirth. Children really aren't on my mind." I say.

"I'm serious." He says with a deep-seated voice.

"Well, I know that a woman heart is sacred. It's more valuable. She's looking for someone to potentially change her name. She's looking for her love to turn her from a woman to a mother. A man only gives his heart to the one he loves. A man would risk his life to make sure his love is okay. It's the lion in him I guess." I say examining every single part of him.

The rest of the day I spent painting, careful not to get paint onto the hardwood floor. Even though my mother is gone, I can still hear her voice in my head. Her voice is guiding my creativity. As I'm painting, I have my door open to air out the paint smell.

Suddenly I could hear my dad coming up the stairs. In my head, I was hoping that he couldn't see me. If only I could be so lucky.

"Amara?" He knocks on the door.

"Yes." I say still working on my painting.

"This next weekend do you want to go out with me?" He says.

"Dad, I'm too old for daddy-daughter dates I have to finish this for art class. I also have a sixteen-page paper due for English." I say turning to face him.

"Oh, okay. Let me know when you're free." He says backing out of my door.

He went into his room soon after. I get up locking the door, choosing to deal with the hard paint smell. I can't help that he loves his friends much more than me. Once I realized that I was able to heal from the pain of him not being there. Even if things for us get better, I will never forgive him for being gone. It would have been better if he had left and started a new family elsewhere, Instead of torturing me for years. My mother warned him about this happening one day. Who would have known my mother would be able to predict the future?

I finally finished my project. The painting took me two weeks to complete. I carefully wrapped the canvas trying to prevent anything from damaging it. Once I arrived at school, I turned my masterpiece into Ms. Santos. I couldn't shake the nervous feeling I had inside.

Each class today was a half an hour long to make room for the assembly. The entire time I was trying to think of something to say when it's my turn to present my painting I was entirely at a loss for words.

English was my last class of the day today. I check in with Ms. Santos before heading to the auditorium. I sit next to Jabari and my friends a nervous wreck waiting to be called. It's moments like this when I love Jabari's animal sense. He was squeezing my hand tight. Which caused me to look at him and slow down my breathing. I sit and watch everyone's performance or presentation. My stomach was in a tight knot, I wasn't this nervous when I did spoken word for the first time. Ms. Santos came and gathered all of us who signed up and walk us backstage. I slowly, but carefully, unwrapped my painting. Everyone who saw it was amazed by it. I stood by the curtain waiting to go onto the stage.

"Next we will have Amara Martin to present to us. Make some noise for Amara." Principal Madison says as she walks away from the center of the stage.

I keep telling myself to breathe, and everything will be fine as I walk to the center of the stage. The lights were brighter than I expected them to be. I pause for a minute and examine the crowd, trying to locate someone I knew. I find Jabari and lock eyes with him. I set my painting on the easel and take the deepest breath of my life.

"I call this piece the King's Golden Queen. This might not look like something that means love, but it does. The lion represents a protector. I used a mixture of browns and blacks for the lion to symbolize his strength. The specks of gold in his mane connects him to his love. The woman has her head, and body facing him because she doesn't fear him. She knows that he will never hurt her. The lion knows that although she is frightened of the idea of love at first, now she understands. Her dark brown skin reflects the gold dress perfectly. Her hand is reaching not to push him away, but to hold him. She often wonders how he could fall in love with someone so lost in the idea of love. The lion wasn't the beast, she was. Thank you." I end nervously and critical of myself during the entire speech.

The entire speech was about my feelings for Jabari. We probably were the only ones who knew that. Everyone clapped for me as I walk off stage. I was the last person to present to the assembly. I went back to my locker to grab my things, but Jabari was at my locker waiting for me.

"That was an interesting speech you gave." He says moving out from in front of my locker.

"Thanks." I say putting my combination in.

"The King's Golden Queen is the perfect name for you, your highness" He says leaning in to kiss me.

We leave school getting into Jabari's car and he takes me home. I'm not good at predicting someone's mood, but Jabari didn't seem okay when he reached the front of my house. He has grips the steering wheel tightly, almost trying not to make eye contact with me. Something was on his mind, he just didn't know how to say it. I place my hand on the back of his neck, pulling him out of his head. In his eyes, I could see fear. This is the first time since I have been with Jabari he's turned back into a boy.

"What's wrong?" I say bending my head to get a better look at him.

"Your description of the painting was about us, wasn't it?" He sighed, grabbing my hand.

"Unintentionally, yes." I became frightened.

"What makes you think you're the beast? I'm the one who transforms into a lion." He clears his throat.

"My idea of love is skewed. It took a lot for me to admit that I love you. You're the first male that has ever shown me love. I had no true male figure in my life. No one else has been able to break my heart like my father has. Once I accepted he would never love me as a father should, I started healing. My father has started the beginning of creating a village of a fatherless child with me." I say looking into his worried eyes.

"I pray that one day as a woman you will be able to find some peace." He says.

"Healing doesn't start until you admit what's causing you the most pain." I say getting out of the car.

I left the painting with Jabari to give to Minnie, although I do love my work. Minnie has a vast collection of different decorations that involve lions. If I were to keep it most likely, it would be lost or damaged. It's too beautiful to just sit in a corner collecting dust. Minnie would take outstanding care of it.

Institutionalized

I thought I would be alone after school because my dad's car was not sitting in the driveway. He was standing by the dining room table yelling at someone on the phone. Just as I closed the door, he hangs up the phone in a fit of rage. I pretend like I didn't even see him and walk upstairs as quickly as possible. When he doesn't drink, he wants to talk.

"Amara! Don't act like you don't see me!" He says stomping up the stairs.

"I had headphones in." I say lying to avoid the conflict.

"You could've waved." He struggles to try to find a reason to yell at me.

"Okay." I say setting my backpack on the floor.

"Amara." He pauses, shaking his head.

"Dad, the truth will always live, it never disappears or passes away." I say taking a seat on my bed.

He walks away not knowing what to tell me. I don't think he understands how sick he is. I'm not a psychologist, but he is definitely mentally ill. Any man or woman who can just abandon their child is sick. If you can enjoy the act of making a child, you can be a decent enough human being to help raise it. Most women don't get the chance to walk away from their child nor has the heart to do it. I know the pain of having a parent just walk away from me. A promise I made to myself when I was a young broken girl is that my child will never have to question my love for them. They deserve the normal I never received.

I'm starting to get burnt out from school. Lately, my fellow classmates have been excited about the fall dance. I have just become so unenthusiastic about almost everything. This morning I had enough time to sit and eat breakfast at the kitchen table. The news anchors were discussing the shooting of an unarmed teenager in Chicago, Pax Willams was his name. I took my focus off of my food and examined the video frame by frame. The car Pax was driving was supposedly stolen. The body camera starts with the police shooting at the vehicle. Pax drives right past them. In my opinion, he was trying to get away. The police were shooting at him while in the car. How was he going to be able to surrender when there were at least seven police officers shooting at him. The new anchor kept saying he was shooting at the police, but given how fast he was driving there was no time for him to pull out a gun.

He ditches the car and starts running. I don't think people realize that he was running for his life. This case ended like every other, shot down like a dog at the end of its life.

Friends and family agree he shouldn't have stolen the car, be he should have never been killed because of it. I understand for police, or anyone operating a gun, it could be impossible for you to shoot someone in the leg while their running. The police say that he was shooting at them, but there were a lot of cops shooting at the car, so how would you know where the gunfire was coming from? I sit back and watch the news anchors try to paint this kid as some low-life gangbanger. Looks like people applauded the police for getting rid of him.

My mother was born and raised on the South Side of Chicago. It's a beautiful city, with beautiful people. The weather was always changing when we would visit family. The one thing I hated the most even though I wasn't being raised there, it's a very segregated city. We would take Lake Shore Drive or the Dan Ryan to reach Downtown. If you pay attention, you can see the transition between rich and poor. Chicago has the largest population of African Americans in the United States. In a city that is struggling to survive this plague of violence amongst citizen, the last thing they need is for the police to have it out for them. The heart of Chicago isn't downtown with the rich, it's in the land of the forgotten people. The heart lives in the ghetto.

I look at the image of Pax Williams and feel disturbed. We will never know the teenager, we will always remember Pax Williams as the unarmed Black kid shot and killed by the police. I couldn't help but think about Jabari. I don't know what I would do if something as tragic as this happened to him.

I'm hoping that English class would be able to cheer me up. I find that I love English class and writing papers because I find that words equal power. I walk into English and take my seat. On the whiteboard in bright blue letters was "discussion" which mean for the next hour we have to sit and listen to each other talk.

"Okay, so today we are going to have an open discussion about your next paper. The topic today is about, how does racism still affect people today? For you to gain points today, you have to contribute to the discussion. I'll have Jason start it off." Mr. Bridges says walking up and down each aisle.

"Uh... there are hate crimes that still happen every now and again." Jason says scratching his head.

"Okay, someone else." Mr. Bridges says looking for someone else to call on.

"Slavery." Maddy raises her hand.

"Explain your thought further." Mr. Bridges says writing on the whiteboard.

"Slaves were taken from Africa and brought here to work in fields. African Americans still receive a lot of racism today." Maddy says.

"Yes! Anyone else just shout it out." Mr. Bridges exclaims.

"There is no such thing as racism anymore. It's a thing of the past. We have had two black presidents since slavery, and there is someone of Hispanic decent running in the upcoming election. To say that there is still racism today is absurd." Andrew points out.

"What in the Jim Crow, did he just say!" I say under my breath.

I roll my eyes in discontent with Andrews's comments, which caught the eyes of Mr. Bridges. Which I can tell he was looking for conflict because his tan skin started to glow with excitement.

"Amara. You look like you have something to say about Andrews comments." He inquires.

"Well, what Andrew said was offensive." I say locking eyes with Mr. Bridges.

"How Amara? I have never seen anything racist happen to a Black person." Andrew scoffs.

"Andrew, you wouldn't know anything about having anything racist happen to you. I hate to bring race into the argument, but you and I have lived very different lives. You wouldn't know about being followed in the store because of your color. Or how people think that you live off of the government. Andrew, you don't see it because it doesn't happen to you. What you say was racism doesn't exist because we have had two African American presidents. It doesn't disappear because someone of African origin was elected. If anything, I saw more racism. They were used as a distraction for African Americans, we were proud to see someone Black have power." I say.

"Amara, I disagree with that statement, I saw more people proud to have some change for once. We do see someone recording a person saying a racial slur, but it happens every once in a while." He says talking with his hands.

"What about there being a higher number of Black people being accused of doing crimes they didn't commit. The person just so happens to fit the description of the suspect. The wrong person was sentenced to serve someone else's crime. Pax Williams was shot dead by the police, he was unarmed. This is America, a beautiful land with great potential and good people. However, with all the good it can't wash out all the blood that has stained its hands. You can't erase the foundation it was built on. " I say looking at him.

"Okay, sorry but police are just doing their jobs. I understand the White people built this country and minorities have the crap end of the stick." Andrew nonchalantly says.

"Yes, you are correct. Not all police are bad. I for one have never had any issue with an officer before. I think that a good officer can make a bad judgment call like everyone else. They're humans with emotions and can't always do the right thing. The issue is that the bad officers are causing harm to the good ones. There are some officers with a God-complex, and that doesn't make them a good person with or without a badge. It also strange in almost every shooting of an unarmed minority the body camera mysteriously stops working. Maybe everyone speaking out about police brutality amongst Black people aren't lying. Fear is the only thing that holds anyone back. Look, we are just tired of it being only our people suffering. Only us being viciously murdered and receiving no justice. The media also plays a huge role on what we see. There were a couple of incidents where the police shot and killed a teenage boy who wasn't Black. The news never covered it, until African American started to talk about it online. That's when it became a huge news story. However, no charges were filed against the officers. Also, if White people built this country like you say, then why did they need to import workers? Just like you can't discover a place where people are already inhabiting. If your ancestors were not lynched, you have no right to tell me as an African American that racism doesn't affect me in modern times." I say sitting up in my seat.

"You're saying that all White people are racist!" He yells.

"Not once in the last fifteen minutes of this conversation have you heard me say anything about White people being racist. I'm merely saying that the system is racist towards Black people. Every single one of us are slaves to a broken system. A system that was meant to fail me as a minority. I follow the routine so effortlessly. I'm a double minority, black, and a female. Sometimes

I don't know which is worst. Racism comes in every single shade including Black. They didn't just lynch Black people, other races were hanging from trees as well. Racist White people make White people who aren't racist look like the whole entire race is prejudice which isn't fair.

"Some White people fight for justice just like us, and they don't get enough credit for doing that. They stand in front of us because they know that nothing will happen to them. Some racist White people feel that they can be discriminated against because they are White. Which I don't understand why they feel that way. It's not fair to say that all White Americans are racist, just like isn't fair for all African American males to be label thugs in the media when they are murdered. As African American how can we say that this country is for us when the slaves never received their reparation. This country promised the slaves forty acres. When America backed out of their promised, it further set the tone of how they view African Americans. Backing out of any promise weather makes a person untrustworthy. Just because something is ended doesn't mean it disappears." I say.

"I'm White, and I don't have prejudice views." He says.

"I never said you did. Every single person, whether they like it or not, has some sort of prejudice view towards another race. There are issues in the Asian, African, Hispanic, and White communities that need to be fixed across the board. People generalize an entire community because they had an issue with someone of that race. The problem is that we are getting away from diversity. This race war that is going on right now came formed in darkness has completely taken over. So many people have lost their lives. How many more will die before we become normal again? Race doesn't matter when we all bleed red. It's not just Black people going through it, immigrants as well." I say.

"Immigration is a huge problem for us. We can't keep allowing people who are not born here to work here illegally." He rebuts.

"Who is illegal on land that is stolen?" I ask.

"What?" He says with a blank stare.

"This land was stolen from a group of people. The people who raped, killed, and tortured the Native American were not born here." I say.

"Things were different back then." He says.

"Oh really, for who? I have seen more violence against people of color in the last two weeks than I have in my entire life. More people are being deported to countries they don't even know how to speak the language. We don't have to agree on everything, but we do need to talk about it. Not talking and staying in separate corners will keep dividing us. The media has a huge impact on dividing us. They chase ratings more than anyone. Unlike the older generation, we know and understand that the media can be one of the biggest liars. The media's job is to create chaos. Just like the rich shouldn't be able to pass laws for the poor. The rich have never lived a poor man's life." I say.

"Amara, if there one thing I can say about you, is that you're definitely not ignorant." He says.

"Look, as long as humans desire wealth, there will always be hate. I don't think your views or my views are wrong. The reason we don't understand each other's point is that we simply live in the same world, but have different lives." I say lifting my shoulders.

"That was the perfect way to end the discussion. Now I want everyone to write down what you thought about Amara and Andrews's debate. Nice job the both of you." Mr. Bridges cheers.

I was kind of happy the debate went as well as it did. Usually, discussions about racism are hardly ever calm, and both sides of the argument get to be heard. My views are different from every other human. A lot of what the slaves went through still affects us to this day as African Americans. I might be the only one that honestly can see the effects of the past still concerning us today. It could just be my brain over analyzing everything that I see. I tend to pay a lot of attention to the world. There is too much good in the world to allow hate to overshadow the good. Andrew was a White male that came from a two-parent household. He has been to over sixty different countries, his parents have a perfect relationship. Andrew is living where he can't see my point of view because he's so blinded by his own. He's been conditioned like the rest of us.

I'm acutely aware of my surroundings, and being around Jabari has caused me to be even more observant. When class ended, Jabari was already waiting for me outside of my class. I think he's become very attached to me. He doesn't act like a regular boyfriend, then again in my life what the hell is normal. It's like we're living in our own world where no one else exists. The good thing is that I haven't forgotten about my friends like some people. Zhivago has respected Jabari ever since their little spat. Today I felt a lot different than usual. I wasn't tired, I had more energy than ever. I felt like I could run a marathon without even trying. The day ended as quickly as it started

The Heavens

It was a gorgeous day today. We sat in Minnie's garden and did homework. I was elated to see my painting hanging on the wall right above the TV. No one was home when we arrived. It feels warm as we were working. Although that could have been the body heat Jabari was giving off that I was feeling. I was working on my statistics homework when I caught Jabari staring at me through the corner of my eye.

"It's not polite to stare at people you know." I laugh moving to the next math problem.

"I'm just looking at God's work of art." He says waiting for me to look up at him.

"Really? Okay." I look at him and laugh.

"Amara, you never talk about your mother." He says changing his facial expression to that of a more serious one.

"I don't know." I say putting my homework down.

"Your heart is beating fast. I'm sorry I made you uncomfortable." He says returning to his homework.

"No, it's okay. I hate that you can hear my heartbeat. What do you want to know?" I say trying to make him feel better.

"Whatever you want to reveal to me." He says putting down his textbook.

"You would have loved her if you met her. She was the best person in the whole world. She was more than just my mother. Her name was Angela Martin, and she was my best friend. Her favorite color was purple, which made it easy when I got her something. The love she had for me I will never get back. A mother's love is once in a lifetime. I will never have anyone to loves me the way she did, unconditionally. When I would be freaking out, she is the one person who would be able to calm me down. We gave each other meaning in our lives. There's nothing she or I wouldn't have done for each other."

"How was she with your dad?" He asks.

"She gave up on him a while ago. My mother wanted to give me the best life possible. If it wasn't for her, he's lucky I even say anything to him when he was home. She never expressed her feelings about him. She told me she never wanted to jump into me and his relationship issues and we have to work it out. He was the white sheep of the black family, to say the least." I say.

"Sounds like she was amazing just like her daughter. She was right to stay out of the fights with your dad." He says.

"He never claimed me. The only time I was ever claimed by him was my eighth-grade graduation. Other than that I was nothing to him. My mother was everything to me and then some." I say.

"You were fortunate." He smiles grabbing my hand.

"The heavens indeed gained an angel when she left. I know that she looks good in her purple wings. I still don't think she understands how much I love her." I say looking up at the sky.

Lions Mane

I finally caved in and agreed to go with Jabari to the dance. I have attended a couple of the school dances, but it has always been with a group of friends. It might be different being that I have a boyfriend. I pick out this beautiful red dress that my mother bought a few years ago, that I never wore. The dress had long sleeves and stopped a little bit below my knees. I had to buy a deep plunge bra because the dress showed a lot of cleavage. There used to be a lot more showing, but my mother sewed it up some. I matched the dress with some red heels that were going to start hurting my feet in about an hour after wearing them. I let my curls out – they were so bouncy. They deserve to have some fun. I sit at my desk in my room and begin to do my makeup. I had just got finished working on my eye when I caught my dad watching me in the mirror.

"Where are you going?" He asks leaning against the door.

"The dance at school." I say gluing on my eyelashes.

"I take it you're going with that boy?" He says.

"Yes, he's my boyfriend." I say searching for my blush.

"You're too young for all that makeup. You should cover up your chest." He says rubbing his face.

"Mom bought the dress for me. Let me ask you something, what did you do when you were younger to women to make God punishing you? I have no idea why he gave you a daughter?" I say putting on my highlighter.

"What are you talking about?" He frowns.

"God gave you a girl to teach you a lesson for breaking a woman's heart. Only a man can cause extreme heartbreak to a woman. It's harder for a man to raise a daughter than a son. Fathers don't spend as much time nurturing their daughters as they would with their son." I say looking at him in the mirror.

"I never broke a woman heart when I was young. You have always been my princess." He says.

"I think the reason you hate Jabari is that fear you have of him doing what you did to a woman in your past." I say putting on my necklace.

155

"Amara?" He shakes his head.

"I know you understand that I'm right. I can see you examining your life. You care more about me now because I have grown into my body. Dad, I'm not your little girl. You're angry with Jabari because you don't want him to undress me and turn me into a woman. Don't worry mom raised me right. I'm not playing the women's game as of yet." I say.

"Amara, I'm sorry." He says choking back tears.

"Me, too." I say putting my lipstick into my black clutch.

"What can I do to fix this?" He says crying.

"When God sends you back judgment day because you didn't learn your lesson. Do me a favor and don't do this to your next daughter in your new life. I have shed too many tears over you. I have none left to cry for you, and I'm sorry. Everything that has happened between you and me is because you didn't care enough." I say putting my heels on.

"Can you give me another chance?" He asks with his shirt soaking up tears.

"I have given you a total of ten chances throughout my life to put me first. You have to seek help dealing with the death of this relationship." I say getting up and turning around.

A parent's worst fear is there child losing faith in them. That's something a parent doesn't want to happen. How does a parent deal with that pain? He will have to deal with that pain. This is the first time we have talked without screaming at each other. He must not be drunk yet being that he was able to hold a conversation with me. I hear Jabari pulling up in the driveway. My dad waits on the couch and watches me walk out the door. I stand at the door for a moment trying to slow down my brain. Not even a doctor can do surgery to fix this broken heart. I know I'm not making it easy on him, but he never made it easy on me. So why should I give him a chance?

I try to walk gracefully to the car to impress Jabari. Although I don't think that I need to do that with him. For him, just the sight of me brightens his day. Jabari looks nice, he had a beautiful black suit. I could tell he put on extra cologne because I could smell it as the wind blew in my direction. He was waiting by the passenger door to open it for me. I wasn't going to fight him, Jabari has been able to soften me a little bit. I didn't grow up seeing my father take charge which is why I tend to take on male traits. He never held the door open for my mother. My dad never bought anything nice for my mother either. A man doesn't need to save me when I can protect myself. As I walk closer to the car, I can see him with the biggest smile on his face.

"You look gorgeous, my love." He says smiling.

"Thank you. You look handsome." I kiss his cheek and get into the car.

It was hard for Jabari to find a parking space, it looked like the whole school was here. We could hear the base from the music outside in the parking lot. The entrance decorations directed us to the gym where the dance was being held. The theme tonight was fire and ice. I was surprised that Principal Madison spent money on an ice sculpture in the shape of two people dancing. The ceiling had a holographic of fire playing. Zhivago and Anne finds us standing over by the drink table. Anne grabs my hand guiding us over to where everyone else is standing in a group by the bubble making machine. Tess and Anne were too busy playing with my hair because it's rare that I wear it all down. They love pulling on my curls stretching them out and watching them bounce back. Anne's hair was naturally wavy because of her Spanish heritage. It looks like she had an ocean on her head. Tess's hair was so straight. It doesn't matter if she puts it up in a bun she will not have a dent. I had to direct them away from my hair to what I was wearing. Every time someone messes with my hair I feel like someone's petting me on my head like an animal. Ethan was so into his phone he didn't even notice. Zhivago couldn't help but undress me with his eyes. He was so glued to me it was hard for him to focus on anything else.

I danced with Jabari the whole night until my heels started killing my feet. The DJ slowed down the music, and Jabari pulls me close to him. I could hear his heartbeat which seems to make mine slow down to match his. At this moment I couldn't help but get lost in his eyes. There is just something about him that makes me feel weightless.

"Amara, I love you." He says.

"I love you, too." I say forcing myself to say it.

"I can tell you just forced yourself to say that." He says taking the lead as we dance.

"Jabari, I do love you." I say.

"Your heart is like the sun rising over Africa in the morning. It's the most beautiful thing in the world, but it takes a moment for it shine light over the land letting everyone know there's a new day." He says spinning me.

"I'm trying not to be a mad Black woman for the rest of my life. I want to get rid of the darkness that is covering my heart. I want to be vulnerable, but something is preventing me from doing that. I don't know what it is." I say looking all over the place.

"Amara, thinking of the torched history of Black people, women would force themselves not to love anyone, even their children, because they would be taken away from them. It's a sad thing that still happens to a lot of Black people today. Men and women are afraid to love because they fear their loved ones leaving them. You're brilliant, you think a lot before you make a decision. I don't blame you. I know you love me, otherwise I wouldn't be this close to you. Amara, you would have shut me down a long time ago." He says.

"Black love can be powerful." I say putting my head on his chest.

"That's because we love harder than anyone else. Our history shows us that." He says.

Instead of driving me home after the dance. I put my black leather jacket on to cover up my chest. Jabari brought me to see Minnie. Every time I see her she's so full of life. She has to be in her late eighties, but she still loves life. Sir was outside walking to the house. It looks like he was returning from being in the woods. Running helps them work out the aggression they continuously have to deal with because of their shapeshifting ability. Like always Minnie had food ready for everyone to eat. She insists I get a bite to eat. Jabari's grandfather watched my every move. I could tell there was something on his mind, whatever it is he's struggling to hold it in.

"Amara, thank you for the painting. It's so beautiful, my friends are jealous. I didn't know you could even paint." She says taking a bite of bread.

"I'm glad you like. I didn't know either until art class." I say picking up the glass of water to drink.

"You're so talented." She says excitedly.

"I hope I find a girl that beautiful." Sir says looking at me.

"Very beautiful." Ekon says.

"Thanks, you two." I say responding to Sir and Ekon.

"Jabari might marry her. I know I would if I had a chance. Amara didn't freak out when she found out he was a lion." Fayden says.

"I would love to have Amara in the family. It would be nice having another girl around." Bejeray says.

"I'm tired of this. Jabari, you will not have this whore in my house again!" Jabari's grandfather says slamming his hands on the table startling everyone.

"Issa! How dare you say that about that girl! Apologize!" Minnie yells at him.

"Granddad! You cannot talk to her like that! I love her. She is a respectable woman." Jabari yells.

"Grandfather, she is a lovely girl. Very smart and well educated. She is someone you would want us to have in our lives." Pharaoh says.

"Look at her! Makeup and black nail polish. Who knows how many guys she been with and you all talk about marriage!" He yells.

"Grandfather, that isn't nice how would you like it if someone were to talk to me like that!" Bejeray yells.

"You can handle yourself Bejeray. Don't forget. You think I forgot what happen to Gregory!" He yells. The name made her fold into her seat.

"It was a joke, granddad! Sir, wasn't being serious!" Jabari screams.

Minnie starts to speak to her husband in Zulu. I sit there feeling embarrassed. Jabari was yelling at his grandfather. The boys just look at me not knowing what to do or say. Bejeray sits in her seat with a blank face, most likely thinking about whoever Gregory is. I reach under the table and start unbuckling my heels so that it would be easier for me to walk home. I walk towards the front door, and before walking out, I decided I need to stand up for myself.

"Issa, you don't even know me. You haven't yet tried to get to know me since I have been around. My mother died a couple a months ago. My father abuses alcohol. I'm not perfect, I have a lot of problem in my life. Jabari is my first boyfriend. I haven't slept with anyone including your grandson. I was groped by a teenager boy at the pool when I was seven. So, intimacy with someone is just not on my mind. Minnie, I'm sorry, but I will not be coming over anymore." I walk out the door.

Jabari runs after me as soon as I walk out the door. I really didn't want to hear anything that he had to say. I just want to walk home and calm down. I know that it wasn't his fault that Issa sees me as an outsider. I can't take what he has says about me to heart. I'm a Black woman. I don't break when under pressure. I might bend, but I will not break. Jabari grabs my wrist trying to stop me from walking home. I quickly push him away from me. He looks at me as he turns around, disappearing into the darkness. I was walking on the road leading back to my home when Jabari pulls up next to me in his car.

"Amara, get in the car. I'll take you home." He says.

"I got two legs with two feet I can walk home. I'll see you later." I say trying not to look in the car.

"Please, I apologize for my grandfather. I will not let you walk all the way home by yourself." He says trying to watch the road.

"I'm good." I say hoping he would leave.

"Please, Amara!" He yells.

"If I get in the car can we sit in silence?" I stop walking and just look at him.

"Yes, please just get in." He sounds relieved when I get in the car.

Jabari obeyed my wishes by not talking to me. Once we reach my house, I get out of the car and slam the door of the vehicle causing the window to shake a bit. I walk quickly to get inside of the house. I know by not saying anything to Jabari he would be hurt. His grandfather didn't care to know my name let alone find out anything information about me. He could have gotten to know me before trying to execute me. I change into sweats and put my blue bonnet on and start writing.

Dear Diary:

The intention for tonight was to have a good time. I'm trying to have a drama free life, but for some reason, I can't seem to get rid of the drama. Issa sees me as a threat, but I'm not. This might break Jabari and me. I don't know, I'm confused at the moment. I don't want to come between him and his family.

~Amara

I lay in bed unable to settle down and fall asleep. My mind wouldn't let me rest. My dad wasn't home, so I sit on the couch flipping through channels hoping that my eyes would become heavy. It was midnight, and if the TV wasn't going to help me fall asleep, maybe looking at the ceiling all night would help. I turn the TV off and start making my way upstairs. There was a knock on the door. I had a feeling it was either my dad drunk or Jabari. I was completely wrong. Pharaoh who seems to now be the person to settle all arguments now.

He walks into the house as smooth as possible. It was the first time that I felt like a little girl who was about to be punished by her parent for being bad. Pharaoh dreads were down and were longer than I thought, he always has them tied back. He took my hand and walks me over to the couch sitting me down. Pharaoh was massive compared to me. He stood in front of me taking a pause before talking.

"I apologize for my grandfather's behavior tonight." He says.

"It's okay you don't have to. You didn't do anything wrong." I spoke in a low tone of voice.

"Amara, the reason he has a discrepancy about this is because he is protecting his family." He explains.

"What? That doesn't make sense. Instead of telling me to stay away he calls me a whore and essentially a low life?" I reply confused.

"He was out of line for that, trust me Minnie is distraught with him. My grandfather just wants to hurt you so you would stay away from us. I changed when I was sixteen and back then no one was able to help me through this. Jabari has trouble controlling it, but around you, he seems to be able to be normal. I'm twenty-five and have been like this for ten years. I'm not always sure if I can control it. I'm jealous of Jabari because he found a way to control it. If given the opportunity I would give anything to be in his position, love is a powerful thing." He says tapping on his right knee looking at me.

"Pharaoh, does it get any easier?" I ask.

"It softens a bit, but we are protectors. That's what drives everything we do. That night in the woods when you were screaming for help. It took everything for me not to kill that man, I had to make sure you were okay first. Our needing to protect takes over, and we can't stop." He says getting up.

"Thanks, Pharaoh." I say.

I ignored every text and phone call from Jabari. I felt a little guilty not picking up the phone. If I have become Jabari's drug, he's sure to be going through withdraw. He might not be able to hold up so good at school today. I don't mean to hurt him, just needing time to think. I left home early today, I needed to print my paper before class. Also giving me the opportunity to avoid Jabari. However, I did text him letting him know that he didn't have to pick me up from my house. Everything Pharaoh told me a couple nights ago has been replaying in my head.

I wait in class nervous to see Jabari. I can handle a lot of things, but for some reason, my mind would not let me move past it. I have my own family issues, and I would hate to become the thing that would break apart his family. Just as I walk into class, I see he was sitting at the desk. I forgot that we had the same class today. So my plan of avoiding him failed.

"Amara, look I'm sorry about what my grandfather said. He was completely out of line for that." He says standing up.

"It's okay. I just was busy trying to work on my homework." I say lying.

"You're lying. I know you are." He says reading through my deception

"A little bit. I'm okay don't worry about it. Please let it go. I don't want to cause a problem with your family. I don't want to come in between you and your family." I say putting my bag on the ground.

"Amara." He says before I cut him off.

"Please for me. Just let it go. Don't tell Pharaoh this but he came and talked to me. I got some clarity. Trust me I understand what you are going through." I say grabbing his hand.

"I have something for you. This necklace is an Ankh which represents life." He puts the necklace around my neck.

"Thank you. This is the symbol that was on your grandfather's hat when I first met him. I have seen in pictures of the ancient Egyptian. What's the difference between this and a cross?" I say examining the wooden necklace.

"Well, this connects us to our African roots. A cross represents death and not too many people know that. The Ankh like Africa, the giver of life." He says smiling.

Slave Plantation

The history of African Americans in a country that doesn't support people of African origin is horrible. I have come to the conclusion that we are not Black American we are Africans who live in America even if we were born here. We as a people spend so much time trying to separate ourselves from our African roots. Africa is the first to create civilization. No matter what country you go to the history of the nation can be traced back to Africa. It sucks that we have to dig so deep just to learn about our own culture. In big cities, we have some communities that Hispanics, Asian, and Middle Eastern live together as a community celebrating their culture. There's not a community where African people can come together and spread love amongst the culture.

It's like we are stuck at the bottom trying to figure our worth as a people. African Americans are stuck to figure out who we are through material things. Gym shoes and cars have brainwashed us to think that those things establish our status. It's almost like Black people have to have a civil war to come together. I can see we are the only group of people that don't trust each other. Black presidents, basketball player, and Black celebrities have been used as symbols to make us feel like we have moved along as a culture. I'm happy that I was able to live to see two men of color as presidents, but I can't help feeling that they were just a part of some big game. Distraction can have severe effects on my civil rights. I feel like I have become a prisoner of war, and no one, not even our own African brothers across the world have come to our aid. I'm not Black, I'm African.

Mr. Bridges' assignment for the class about racism in today's society has my brain running a marathon. I have much knowledge on the subject, it's a shame to be only limited to ten pages. This topic is much more than a paper it's a movement. I could mention the pro-Black protest. Many people confuse pro-Black as being a racist protest. But it's nowhere as near as racist as it could be. The problem I have with Black protest is that we just protest. Nothing ever happens when we protest. Black movements will always come and go. I question do they ever really accomplish anything? Too many people are afraid to go to jail for what they believe in. If you don't break the law, you won't change the law.

Many political activists of the past were not worried about going to jail. It was easier back then I guess. The new Negro does understand that not fighting gives political leaders the opportunity to undo the work of achieving civil rights. There have been so many lives lost, and we seem to be moving backwards. I might as well have a chain around my neck.

I think Mr. Bridges underestimated the complexity of the assignment, especially for someone like me who is passionate about the topic. The topic of racism has a lot of layers. In each presidency, African Americans issues are put on the back burner all the time. It's like we're on the playground and are still waiting to get our turn on the swing. Everyone keeps jumping in front of us. Maybe I could pick Jabari's brain and have a discussion with him. I could just be being Amara and over thinking everything, but I realize not thinking has gotten us in this predicament we are in now.

I rode on Jabari's back as he took us deep into the woods later that evening. There was a blanket already set up for us to sit. We sat comfortably close to the waterfall. I had never seen a place more beautiful in my life, especially in this small little town. I took my notebook out of my backpack and I waited for Jabari to come back to being human. He took the bag stuffed filled with his clothes behind the tree.

"I need help doing my English paper." I say looking for a pen.

"The great Amara needs help doing her paper? I don't believe that." He kisses me and laughs.

"Well, I don't really need help. I more so need help organizing my thoughts and since you need help with math. I think this more of a trade." I smile.

"Fair enough, so what do you need help with?" He grabs his math homework out of my backpack.

"Mr. Bridges prompt, 'How does racism still affect people today?' What I'm struggling with is organizing my topics." I say.

"That's a very complex topic. There are a thousand points that you can bring up." He says.

"I feel that it never went away, and racism is just as bad as before. Okay for instance if I want to move to an area where there are very few African American, they use real estate tactics to make sure I can't move there." I say.

"Not only that but a lot of the time they will look at where a person's priorities are. Some African males tend to by a car before they think about buying a home. That can deny them being able to buy a home along with racism." He says.

"Some people would like for you to see what they're riding instead of see then there home." I say taking notes.

"So, when they're denied, they're left in a very improvised area left to figure out another way." He picks up his calculator.

"We don't have the necessary resources to sustain our people. You would think that Black celebrities would help us. They too were in our positions at one point in time." I say searching for my highlighter.

"If a poor Black person becomes rich most of the time they turn their back on us poor Black folks. Black celebrities don't give back to the community unless there is some sort of natural disaster. Even though Black celebrities' biggest supporters are Black people. We are the reason they have millions of dollars." He says.

"It not their faults if you think about it. They can't risk looking too African. Looking too Black can ruin their careers. They can help the community a lot with their money." He says.

"No one Black and influential will leave Hollywood clean. Seems as though the system just won't let us have anything to be proud of. Either they're going to kill your career while you're alive or ruin your legacy when you're dead. The dead can't defend themselves. I don't think the slaves understood how badly they were hurt." I say looking at the math problem he was stuck on.

"What do you mean?" He says staring at me as I'm trying to solve the problem in my head and have the conversation.

"The slaves were never given the opportunity to deal with their mental pain of them being forced to work. Think about it, Black people had to prove that we are human. They were denied the opportunity to read. They were beaten worse than dogs. The slaves praised there oppressor out of fear. After slavery, power no longer had a face. Africans were brought here to serve. They never intended for them to be humans with rights, the slaves wanted to move away from claiming to be African. Hair dye, relaxer, flat ironed hair, you name it all moves us away from our true identity." I say handing him back his notebook with steps on how to solve the problem.

"Explains why we can't have any commitment to each other. People are trying to erase their African identity. If you disown your culture and anything related to it the better off you are." He says looking confused at the steps.

"We have been conditioned to believe that Africa isn't worth claiming." I say.

"Yeah, most people don't understand the issue with self-hating." He says.

"It's sad that Africa has the most natural resources, but yet their people are suffering." I glance over at the waterfall.

"You know what the problem is we don't have an African bank. If you're not backed up by the bank, you have nothing." He scoffs.

"You're right." I say returning his homework.

"Black people can never be deported to Africa because we were forcibly brought here. There is no connection to the country for us." I say shrugging.

"If you can't be deported then what happens?" He asks.

"You're put in jail." I say looking at him.

"Exactly!" He shouts.

"Petty offenses become major felonies. Those men and women are put away for the rest of their lives over minor offenses." I yell feeling the anger rise up in me as I think about our injustices.

"Correct. Jail works just like the slave ship. If you keep them locked away, they stay chained on the ship. The term 'African

American' has only existed for about 38 years or more. Technically it's still a very new term." He recounts.

"Racism is like an incurable disease." I say.

"Also, notice how as a culture we will go to church every Sunday and give our money but the church never gets involved in social issues of the community. I have yet to see a church stand up and stand with the community." He says.

"Well, it's church." I say confused where he was going with his point.

"Black people praise God, as he should be. He is the Omega and should be commended for creating life. However, the Black church stays out of issues affecting the very same people who come every Sunday giving them money. The church for Black people is the foundation of the community. It's not far of a reach to say that they are paid to keep silent. If the Black church were involved, we would have a good start to change. The church had a huge impact on the civil rights movement." He says.

"Not only that but they gave God a face. The Omega should never be given face by the White man. He should be in the air and in the plants. He's everywhere, he doesn't need a face and skin color. You tell everyone else they're beneath you because God is our skin color. We're a disorganized group of people. We don't commit to each other. So many of our people try to break away from being African. I don't think we will ever be able to heal as a people." I say

"Disorganized to be reorganized. In the future, we can only hope that more people see the problem like we do, and then change can happen. Hopefully, our people will stick to trying to change and not let any movement die off like all the other ones." He says.

"The hunted will become the hunter. The prey will always outsmart the hunter, the prey is never weak." I say hoping he got that I was using a lion reference.

"Well, the prey has a lot of catching up to do." He laughs.

"One more question who is Gregory?" I ask.

"You have a brain of an elephant." Jabari laughs as he sees I let nothing get by me. "Gregory was Bejeray's soon to be husband. He was tall, short hair, lifted more weights than any of us. Bejeray didn't tell anyone of us that she had changed. She hid it for a couple months. When she would visit us, she acted like everything was normal. Two years ago, she and Gregory wanted to have some fun if you know what I mean. She couldn't control all of her emotions. Her hormones took over, Gregory went flying across the room. Bejeray put him in a coma for three months. He lived, but he didn't remember who she was. After that, she confessed everything. She was the second to experience the change. That's why we are not supposed to fall in love, because if that happens, we cannot control our emotions." He says trying not to make eye contact.

"That's why Pharaoh didn't want me around. He doesn't want anything to happen to me." I say looking at Jabari becoming uncomfortable telling me the story.

We stayed in the woods studying and I continue to pick his brain. It was nice being able to have someone who's equally smart as me. We both seem to have knowledge on a very controversial topics. We talk for hours about it but couldn't seem to come up with a solution to a never-ending problem. Will there ever be a solution to end racism? I can't answer that nor can he.

The Savanna

The love of my life is not human, he's something else more significant which scares me. When I'm around him, I feel like nothing else in the world matters. I almost feel weightless, or like I can fly if I wanted to. He's becoming much more than my boyfriend. Jabari has become my protector. If I were about to be run over by a car, Jabari would risk his life to save me. I would do the same for him.

Jabari is a good person I don't want to ruin him by being so selfish all time. I feel like I'm using him in a way. Not using him in the sense that I'm trying to gain something from him. I'm using him to get stability in my sad little life. He's become the light at the end of an icy and dark cave. I feel like I haven't given him anything back in return. He's helping me see myself and the world around me differently. Lately, I have been so aware of everything that is going on around me that I have been evaluating myself. Once you start paying attention to your surroundings, you can never turn it off. I have become extremely aware of the world.

Mr. Bridges assignment was supposed to be ten pages. I had so much information on this topic I ended up writing a twenty-page paper. I turned it in two weeks ago but still haven't received any feedback on it. The rest of the class has their grades and feedback but not me. I knew that it was long, but it's going on three weeks and still nothing which is concerning. I'm hoping he didn't lose the paper and is giving me a low grade because he lost it. After class ended, I decide to talk to Mr. Bridges, to get some sort of an update and not be so in the dark.

"Mr. Bridges, do you have a second?" I walk up to his desk.

"Yes of course. What is on your mind?" He says erasing the board.

"It seems as though the rest of the class has received their essays back and I haven't. It's going on three weeks. I have yet to hear anything following the essay." I say.

"Oh, yes, here you go." He searches for the paper in a stack of graded papers and proceeds to hand it to me.

"Thank you." I look down at the paper and am shocked. "What?! A zero?!" I look up at him waiting on an explanation.

"Yes, it is an exceptionally written paper, but not factual." He says walking behind his desk.

"I have resources! There a bibliography attached to the paper." I say.

"Yes, I saw that. What I'm trying to say is that your paper sound very pro-Black. You don't really talk about anything that happens to people of other races." He explains.

"The paper was mainly opinion based, and we didn't need to include resources. I included some just in case. I have been living as an African America for eighteen years. I can't talk about how people from Mexico risk their lives every day trying to cross the board to get into this country to work so they can provide a better life for their families. They're treated like crap and are told even if they're not Mexican to go back to Mexico. I also can't talk about the Asian kid whose so focus on school because his parents are so hard on him about getting into an Ivy League school. His parents don't want him to become like them overworked and tired. Using scare tactics to make them choose schooling over anything else. Mr. Bridges, pro-Black doesn't mean anti-any other race. It just means that I'm happy about being born African I want the best for my race. Pro-Black means I want to encourage economic growth of African Americans. I touched on racism within the community." I say.

"I understand that, but there is a way to go about doing things, and this isn't it. You have the highest-grade average in the class so one bad grade will not affect you that much." He sits down at his desk.

"That not the point, you're telling me that my opinion doesn't matter. The paper was opinion based. You're not understanding my frustration." I say.

"Amara, there's another paper coming up you can redeem yourself. Now go before you're late to your next class." He says folding his arms.

This was complete bullshit! I was so pissed leaving Mr. Bridges class today. He was telling me something that was based on my opinion was wrong. I have probably written hundreds of papers over four years in my high school career. This paper was the best thing I could have ever worked on. I went to my locker and exchanged out my textbooks. I slam my books into my locker, and shortly after Jabari shows up out of nowhere.

"What has the young lioness upset?" He asks.

"Adults that are in their late forties that have a receding hairline, who always smells like a pack of cigarettes and six gallons of coffee." I say furiously searching for my calculator.

"Okay, you have described half the male teachers here. Which particular one are you talking about?" He queries picking up the pens that have fallen out my locker.

"Mr. Bridges basically told me my paper was too Black. I now have a zero on my paper that I worked extremely hard on." I say almost turning red.

"That sucks what are you going to do about it?" He says.

"I don't know, but I will not back down from this!" I say.

"You're a woman. God gave each the ability to stand their ground. He made the Black women the toughest thing on the earth. By the way, do you still have the recording of the Biology lecture from last week? I'm having trouble identifying cells." He says redirecting my focus off of my English paper.

"Yeah." I say.

I pull out my tape recorder still recording as we spoke. Which means that I was still recording my conversation with Mr. Bridges. I look at Jabari twisting the thought around in my head what I could do if in fact Mr. Bridges was recorded on tape denying me my grade because it's too Black. I'll just have to stop by Principal Madison's office and talk to her about this. I tried to do things the easy way, but sometimes the harder way is much better for people to understand not to mess with your hard work. There is only one thing that I remarkably take pride in, which is my school work. My mother instilled in me the power of being able to learn. It's my job to make sure that my school work is turned in on time and as correct as possible.

The entire day I toyed with the recording. Trying to figure out how I wanted to go about it with Principal Madison. I walk to the principal offices and stop outside of the door. What if there was another way to handle this, I think. I sit anticipating the sight of Principal Madison to make her appearance. The receptionist Jean checks me in. There was no one else in the office, so the old wooden chair made a loud sound as I sit down.

Principal Madison walks out of her office in a black dress with a pink blazer with red heels. She was a Black woman so I was hoping that she would be able to understand why I'm agitated. She walks with such grace and excellence, her hips move as she walks.

"Amara, nice to see you! Come into my office." She says standing tall over me.

I get up and walk into her office. This was my first time being in the principal's office. Like every other Black child, I grew up with the fear of my mother and what she would do to me if I got in trouble at school. If there's one fear that African Americans, all share is the fear of our mothers. I made sure that I did everything in my power not to get in any sort of trouble at school because I knew who I had to come home too. The office, although relatively big, seemed small because of all the piles of paperwork that was everywhere. I don't think that her desk could hold another piece of paper even though it was solid wood. It still might break in half. The office was painted a light green color with white accent décor.

"Amara, what brings you to my office?" She asks.

"Mr. Bridges wanted us to talk about how racism still affects people in modern times. I just received my paper today, and it was given a score of zero." I say.

"Well did you talk to Mr. Bridges?" She ask moving forward in her chair.

"Yes, he told me the paper was pro-Black, and it wasn't acceptable. The paper was opinion based, and he essentially told me that I was wrong. I highlighted the positive and the negatives of the community. I have the recording to prove it. I talk about what I know happens to Black people in this country." I say.

"Amara, I'm going to have to investigate this. If you have your essay with you right now, I will take it and read it over." She says.

I felt good handing over my paper to Principal Madison. Hopefully, this situation will be handled smoothly. I meet up with Jabari as he waits in the front of the parking lot for me. There was a look on his face that I knew all too well. There was something on his mind he wanted to say to me. I give him a hug, and he kisses me on my forehead. Once I settle into my seat of his car, the questioning begins.

"The last time you were over my house you say you were touched as a child by a boy." He says not wanting to ask.

"I did say that. That was the first time I ever said that out loud." I say thinking back to that night.

"Amara, have you seen a therapist?" He asks as he was pulling out of the parking lot.

"No." I say.

"You really should. That's a traumatic thing that happened to you. I'm surprised your parents didn't talk to you." He says.

"They didn't know. I never told anyone." I fold in the seat.

"What?! Why didn't you tell them?" He asks.

"I don't know. It doesn't bother me." I say.

"You may think that, but it explains a lot about you." He says.

"What do you mean?" I ask.

"When it comes to males it's hard for you to become comfortable around them. Part of that might have something to do with your father, but some of that could be you being touch. You're harder on males than with females. I thought it was just because you were just a dominant female, which I like. I understand you a bit more now." He says glancing at me.

"What are you my therapist now?" I question.

"I'll be whatever you need me to be." He says cracking a smile.

"I just might take you up on that offer." I say watching him drive.

"I'm not taking you home just yet there somewhere we need to stop first." He looks at me.

I look out the window, and instantly knew where he was taking me. He's stubborn like me, which is why he was going against my word and taking me to his house. A part of me wanted to yell at him, but I was going along with his madness at the moment. I know that he has a good heart.

When we arrived at the house, I really didn't feel like getting out of the car. I haven't been over for such a long time that the house felt strange to me. Jabari walks over to me grabbing my hand dragging me into the house. No one was home other than Issa. He was sitting at the kitchen table, watching me as I walk through the door. I didn't want to be here in the first place. Issa is the last person I wanted to see.

"Hello, Amara." Issa says looking at Jabari and back at me.

"I asked my grandson to bring you over today. I want to apologize for my behavior a couple of weeks ago." He says folding his hands

"Okay?" I say feeling like I was being set up.

"I wanted to drive you away because you reminded me of the Goddess Oya. When my family talks about you, I noticed that you share so many of the same traits as her. I see in you what my grandson sees, you can bring people to the darkness and show them light. You are a warrior and a protector. Sometimes it takes a storm to see the light. Please accept my apology." He gets on his knees and bows to me.

"I accept." I say helping him up.

I was confused about what Issa was saying to me. I help him back into the chair and walk outside. Jabari needs to help my brain decode what Issa was talking about. He was laughing as we walk back to the car. I watch, waiting for him to say something before I need to ask.

"So are you going to explain what your grandfather just said?" I ask waiting for a response.

"You have energy around you that only can be Oya, the Orisha of wind and storm. Bejeray was the first person to notice those similarities. Once she said something I started paying attention to you. Every time I see you, you're wearing this copper bracelet. You never back down when challenged. Take your mother for example. Her favorite color was purple, she was born in September which is the ninth month. Oya's favorite number is nine. Purple and marron are her favorite colors just like your mother. Amara Storm Martin is your full name. Literally, your middle name is Storm, it doesn't get any clearer than that. Oya is showing you the signs that she is around you. Amara, you just have to listen and work with her." He jumps around.

"Okay, this bracelet was a gift from when I was younger. The things about my mother I have no control over. I'm starting to believe in signs." I say looking at events in my life since birth.

"My grandfather would hear us talk about you, and he reminded us of Oya. She brings change with every storm, which is why he fears her. Anytime it rains or a storm of some type that is Oya's doing. You could very much be a child of Oya." He smiles.

As Jabari was driving me home, it begins to rain, and I slowly get a headache. I'm starting to believe Jabari and Issa. Oya could be showing me signs now that I'm older and can understand her. Now I'm going to pay more attention to the signs. I'm ready to receive the information from her if she is willing to give it to me.

Sahara

Ms. Maddison pulls me into her office during lunchtime. When I walk into the office, Mr. Bridges was sitting in one of the seats. I sit in the chair next to him. He looks very much upset, to the point that he was turning bright red. I try to act surprised the reason as to why I was here, but I knew why.

"Mr. Bridges, it has come to my attention that you gave Amara a zero on her paper about racism." She says with her hands folded on the desk.

"Yes, I gave her a low grade because the paper didn't correctly cover racism. It covered racism within the African American community." He stutters.

"I have read over her paper. Before I was a principal, I taught English for six years. Her paper adequately discusses the effects of systemic racism amongst the Black community. Why exactly did you give her a low score?" She asks.

"Well, Amara's paper talks about racism within the African American community. That wasn't what the paper was supposed to be about. The paper was supposed to cover racism between two ethnicities. For example Blacks and Whites." Mr. Bridges explains.

"I'm afraid you're wrong. Amara perfectly explained how systematic racism has caused African Americans to hate each other. Amara explains how Black people will not hire within their own race. Which is true, growing up I was told by my parents that you can't do business with Negros. My grandparents taught that to my parents which they passed down to me." She says.

"Well..." Mr. Bridges was at a loss for words.

"Not only that, she addresses how skin and hair affect causes Black women to hate each other. I hear it from most of the young Black girls here. Their standards of beauty have been hurt because of the older generation. If you are nappy, you're not right. Straighter hair is more acceptable in the workplace and in school. There have been young African American women suspended because they wore protective styles. That type of thinking has held up in the South back when the older generation used to work on farms. That teaches young girls they will never be anything because of their hair. Those teachings are passed down to their children and so forth. Lighter skin is more praised than darker skin. Movies would rather hire lighter skinned women and men to play their roles. Darker skin is only used to play slaves when needed. Lighter skin women don't realize they have light-skinned privilege. Most makeup brands don't believe that dark can sell which hurts the younger girls that see that. Some African Americans try to claim they're biracial to escape their African identity. Also, African American women are seen as monsters for being born with large butts. It's ugly on us but beautiful of the opposite race. African American women are killing themselves to win in this deadly competition with each other. Those are just some of many points she has made." Principal Madison leans forward onto her desk.

"I could regrade her paper." Mr. Bridges say while turning to look at me.

"I already have, Amara will be receiving a score of one hundred percent. Her paper should have been scored on the structure and not opinion. Not letting a child question the way things are limits them, making them robots to a heartless system.

Amara's thoughts are to be heard not silenced. God is the spiral, he is the only one who can judge." She glances over at me.

"Okay." He says surrendering.

"Amara, you can head to class, lunch will be ending soon." She smiles.

I walk out of that office feeling like I have been heard. There was a part of me that hated that I got Mr. Bridges in trouble, but my opinion will always matter. The problem is people have been so set in our own thoughts sometimes forgetting we are limiting learning. If you don't question why things are structured the way they are you will never be able to understand. Education comes from gaining, thinking, and listening to someone else's ideas. Obtaining knowledge never stops.

The school decides to give the seniors a lesson in safe sex. I think it's too late to give a lesson on how to protect yourself with seniors. It is uncomfortable sitting next to a bunch of teenagers who, for most of them, have already had experienced that part of their life. The senior class was about one hundred students. There wasn't an even number of females to males. The boys were joking around the entire time. We are about twenty minutes into an hour lecture, and ten guys have already been kicked out. It's hard for everyone not to laugh. However, the auditorium was completely silent when the video of a woman giving birth came on. I have never seen so many people turn pale.

At the end of the lecture, as we walked out of the auditorium, they passed out contraceptives to the students. I walked out with Anne laughing pulling out some of the condoms and blowing them up. Zhivago and Eric were throwing them at each other. I walk to my locker gathering my things to get ready to go for the day.

"So, Amara have you and Jabari done it yet?" Anne starts to play in my hair messing up my braid out.

"No, and don't touch my hair. It makes me feel like I'm some kind of wild animal." I snatched my now tangled hair out of her hands.

"Why not? You guys have been together long enough." She says looking into my locker.

"Our relationship is not like the average one. It a lot more complicated." I try to skip around her question.

"Don't you love him?" She jumps.

"Yes." I yell.

"So why haven't you guys done it yet!" She yells.

"Our relationship is based on knowledge. Yes, we are attracted to each other, but what attracts me to him is his way of thinking." I close my locker and look her in the eyes.

"Okay, if you say so." She smiles.

There is no exact way to tell your friends that your boyfriend can transform into a lion. The conversation with Anne was just awkward. I haven't really thought about it. I'll experience things in time. Jabari took me home, but we couldn't hang out. He had an awful day at school today and needed to go for a run. I might not see him tomorrow, when he's agitated, sometimes it can take him days to calm down. Once home I went up to my room and put the condoms that the school gave me and put them in my dresser drawer where I keep my t-shirts. I don't plan on using them anytime soon so they should be safely hidden in my clothes.

Dear Diary:

What is a woman to do when the man she loves isn't even a man at all? It's hard sometimes to ignore the little part of him that isn't human. I don't know exactly what happened that has him so upset. The entire car ride he didn't want to talk, and if he did, he just grunted the whole time. I know that he will never intentionally hurt me. Even though I don't have to worry, it's always best not to put all of your trust into someone. People have murdered their own children for less.

~Amara

The King Is Dead

I feel like I know so much about Jabari, but yet so little. He loves to pick my brain and find out all of my secrets. When I ask him, he dodges around the questions sometimes. I allow him to do that to make him feel comfortable. A relationship foundation is built on trust. I trust him with all my life and being that he could potentially kill me if he becomes upset I tread lightly, using wisdom. It's like he has become a piece of steel I can't break or cut. It has become his hobby to try and help me solve my problems. Although that's because of the non-human part of him won't allow him to be away from me too long. I'm pretty sure he sneaks into my house every night to make sure I'm still breathing.

Today was a different type of day, he's taking me to our secret place deep into the woods. I rode on his back until we reach the clearing where the waterfall and the trees connect. I jump off his back and set up a blanket while I wait for Jabari to change back into his regular form. It was a surprisingly hot day, I figure we would eventually get into the water. Once Jabari comes out from behind the trees as himself I was happy to see him. I wait a couple of minutes before I pounced on him with questions.

"Tell me about your feelings." I ask.

"What do you mean?" He says.

"Black men don't express their feelings. You don't want anyone to know your pain. Me being a Black woman I tend to forget that Black men carry around pain too. It's usually all about me. It's a flaw amongst us. We have this wall around us that can cause us to make men suffer because of someone else who damaged us. A Black man has no friends that he can break down, cry, and scream or do whatever he needs to do to let the pain go. You hold it in and let it buildup. Then lash out because you were programmed not to show any emotion. Jabari, don't hide your feelings from me." I step in front of him and grab both of his hands.

"Amara, you wouldn't understand." He says.

"I'm your girlfriend you have become my diary with endless pages. Why can I not be yours?" I grab his hand.

"Okay, there are times that I feel like I can hear my ancestors talking to me. The voices of other members of the tribe can be so loud at times. This gift that I have is also cursed at the same time. When I change sometimes, it feels so good that I don't want to go back to being on two feet. I'm scared that I like being on four. It's much more pleasing and empowering. I replay in my head the thought of hurting you because if we get into a fight and I lose it. Amara, I don't want to kill you. My one fear is watching you die in my hands. I don't want to be the reason you die. Amara what if we get into a fight. I could kill you instantly." He let's a tear roll out of his eyes.

"It wouldn't be the first time I looked death in the face." I hug him.

When I arrive back home, my dad walks outside yelling at me to get into the house. When he's sober, he uses his brain. I hop out of the car as quick as possible. I tell Jabari to hurry up and leave. Between school and him finally opening up to me about his emotions, everything is all over the place. Right now, Jabari is a ticking time bomb.

My dad walks down the stairs waiting for me.

"Get your ass in the house!" He yells.

"Why are you yelling?" I was confused.

"You are not to see that boy again!" He yells slamming the door.

"Why?" I say setting the wet towel on the chair.

"This is why!" He throws the condoms that I got from sex education at me.

"Why were you in my room?" I scream while pacing back and forth.

"It's my damn house! I can go anywhere I want." He screams knocking over the glass on the table.

"Okay, but why did you go through my drawers." I examine the once put together cup now shattered.

"I was being nice and putting your things away, and I saw these. You are not allowed to see that boy again. I don't want no

babies to be running around here. I had a fish dream the other day."
He says.

"Dad, they handed those out at the end of our mandatory sex education class. You can ask the school if you don't believe me. I don't know why you had a fish dream I'm not pregnant." I yell.

"Why did you keep these then? Are you still my little girl?" He asks.

"Why is everyone so concerned about me and what's attached to my body but me? I will never be your little girl. You played the field my entire life. Go seek help so you can heal. I'm fine with where we are now." I run up the stairs slamming my door.

I need everyone to stop worrying about me. I'm in control of my life. I feel like there is a wall that is caving in on me. The best thing for a person is to be themselves and never apologize for it. I know that he thinks that he's protecting me, but he isn't. He's only furthering the wedge in our relationship. My dad tells me that he loves me, but I'm lying when I respond back to him. I can't tell someone I love them when there's no connection with us. My mother has borne him a child so why does he hate me.

The next day at school I try to shake off the evening. I hadn't seen Jabari yet. I make my way to class and sit down listening to the assignment. Just my luck, I was assigned to a project with Zhivago, which when Ms. Santos announced we were partners he smiles from ear to ear. The assignment involved two minds coming together. Ms. Santos is a very hippy teacher and doesn't always give the best guidance when she hands out assignments.

"Amara, do you want to come to my house this weekend? We could start brainstorming." Zhivago holds the door for me as we walk out of class.

"How about we meet up at the library? We could examine the art textbooks to get an idea." I try to get out of going over to his house.

"Oh, okay." He response disappointed.

"Yeah, I'll text you later so we can talk about it." I say spotting Jabari in the distant.

Zhivago has always been my friend, but ever since Jabari moved here, he's making me feel uncomfortable. The two were indeed opposites of each other. Jabari was calmer, while Zhivago lets anything just fly out of his mouth. His skin complexion was like mine except his was smoother, kind of like peanut butter. Zhivago's hair was in a high-top fade. I know what he wants from me, but I just can't give that to him. I value our friendship much more. Maybe in another lifetime, I could try things with him, but even then, I'll still be thinking about Jabari. I have become like many other females who fall in love. Love makes you blind, but I still need to be able to see to drive.

"Hey, I can't hang out with you this weekend." I try to sound sweet while telling him.

"Are you locking yourself in the house this weekend?" He laughs setting the bottle of water he was drinking on the floor.

"I got partnered with Zhivago for the next art project. I'm going to meet up with him at the library this weekend." I say hoping that he wouldn't freak out. When I spoke his name there instantly was a coldness that came over him.

"Okay." He sighs with disapproval.

"I know. Just trust me." I say.

"I do trust you, it's him I don't trust." He says looking visibly upset.

The weekend arrived just as fast as the week began. I walk to the library and wait for Zhivago to get there. There was barely anyone in the building to consume the space. My bag made a huge sound when it hit the ground. It was about half an hour before Zhivago showed up. I had almost three pages full of notes. He pulls the chair as close to me as possible, to the point where I could feel his breath against my cheek.

"So, Amara what are your ideas?" He asks pulling out his supplies.

"The concept I was thinking of was sun and a moon. However, I had an even better idea if we were to split the canvas in half and we each do our own thing. Two worlds coming together as one." I show him some ideas I wrote down.

"Okay, cool. I'll start painting first, and when I finish it's all yours." He smiles.

We were at the library for about three hours just picking each other's brains for ideas. Zhivago walks me home from the library. It was nice hanging out with him again. I have been so in my own world that I tend to forget that other people exist. Zhivago and I were three doors down from my house when he reaches out to hold my hand. I instantly pull my hand out of his.

"Zhivago, what are you're doing you know I have a boyfriend." I say.

"So, I still can't hold your hand?" He pretends like he was confused.

"Zhivago, you can't do that. I'm in love with Jabari" I stop walking.

213

Before I could even finish my sentence, Zhivago pulls me into him kissing me. I get out of his grip and slap him in the face. I was pretty sure Jabari was close by watching and waiting for me to get home. I check the bushes to make sure that there wasn't a huge lion coming out ready to attack.

"Zhivago, you are way out of line for that!" I walk fast away from him.

I was so upset with him. I couldn't believe what had just happened to me. Zhivago forced himself on me, sticking his tongue into my mouth. I run upstairs into the bathroom and rinsed my mouth out with so much mouthwash the bottle was empty. That was the easy part, the hardest part was going to be telling Jabari and praying that he could contain himself. In the midst of all my confusion, somehow, I was able to compose myself. I run downstairs, and out the door. I knew that I wouldn't be able to sleep knowing what has happened. Jabari has to know what happened.

I walk as fast as I could over to his house almost in a running motion. Outside of the home seemed so peaceful, that was all about to change in a minute. I was about to knock on the door, but Pharaoh opened the door before I could. He pushes me back out of the doorway.

"Amara, you need to go. Now isn't a good time for you to be here." He says rushing me down the steps.

"I need to talk to Jabari. It's important! It can't wait." I yell.

"Amara!" Jabari yells from inside of the house. He came outside in a fit of rage. I was so confused as to why he was so upset with me. Jabari looks ten times bigger than usual.

"I need to talk to you." I say slowly backing up.

"How could you!" He yells.

"How could I what?" The puzzles in my head where not fitting together.

"Sir, was out running passed your house. He saw you kissing Zhivago." He yells.

"I didn't kiss him he kissed me. I ran over here to tell you what happened! It's a misunderstanding! I swear on my life!" I yell glancing at everyone on the porch.

"I'll come back later when you have calmed down and are able to talk to me. I didn't do anything to hurt our relationship." I turn around and start to make my way back home.

"Jabari! No! Stop!" Pharaoh shouts.

I turned around to see a massive lion running I knew that standing in front of Jabari like this can get me killed. At this point in my life, it really doesn't matter since my mother has been gone nothing else can take the wind out of me. I knew the amount of love Jabari has for me even as angry as is he wouldn't allow him to hurt me. He ran to me in a fit of rage, letting out a deep roar before he stopped right in front of me growling, digging his claws into the dirt.

"You are a Black man. Angry. It can consume you if you let it. I'm not the enemy. I am a woman who loves you and only you. The rage you're feeling right now can kill you, like it has every other Black male growing up in improvised areas. I'm with you because I see the change you are trying to make. If you're going to kill me, you might as well. You have to die for what you love in order to live." I say looking at a lion in his eyes.

Jabari realized the mistake he has made. I don't know what he was thinking. I'm pretty sure that if he hadn't calmed down, he could have killed me, his worst fear would have become a reality. He slowly backs away, ashamed of himself. He runs as fast as he could disappearing into the woods. I look at everyone on the porch in horror of what could have happened. The look on Minnie's face was that of fear. Even from far away I could see the fear in her eyes. Bejeray drops to the floor probably having a flashback to the night she almost killed Gregory. I lock eyes with Pharaoh, his face says it all. He walks back into the house grabbing the key to his truck. This is one conversation with Pharaoh, nor I didn't want to have, but I knew I had to.

War Diamond

I felt sick. Sicker than I have ever been in my entire life. My stomach felt like it was in a knot. Jabari has to be upset with himself right now. Pharaoh walks over to me and guides me to his truck. I don't think I was breathing the entire time. The problem I have now is knowing where we go from here now. My life is not a story I can just write. Life is supposed to be hard otherwise you're not learning anything, but what is the lesson to be learned here? Pharaoh didn't look like he wanted to talk to me. He tried to avoid making eye contact with me. Plus, it started to rain, which made looking out the window unpleasing. I guess Oya was working her magic. Lighting can be beautiful and dangerous.

"I know you can hear him. What is he saying?" I fold.

"You don't want to know. Jabari just upset with himself. He could have killed you tonight. He has to deal with what could have happened." Pharaoh looks concerned.

"I know." I mumble under my breath.

"Amara, why didn't you back down? Runaway, I mean." He asks.

"I told you when we first met. I don't back down easy or give in easily. Plus, you can't outrun a pissed off lion." I look at him.

"Amara, you are not alone." Pharaoh says.

"Sometimes you have to be the lone wolf. Being alone gives you the chance to think for yourself. Think about the things you have done. It's better to be alone than to be the weakest member of the pack or in this case the weakest lion." I look into his big brown eyes.

Pharaoh assured me that everything was going to be okay. I highly doubt that things are going to be back to normal. You have to be aware of every single thing you do because of the history of our people. I'm trying not to let my pride get me killed or anyone else. As soon as we pulled up to my house, I was gathering my things to go inside my house. I was two second from stepping out of the truck before Pharaoh grabs my wrist. He didn't say anything to me, he couldn't, what more was there to say? We just looked at each other for a minute, no words were spoken. He let my wrist go, I got out his truck. I could see my dad in the window watching me. He opens the door for me.

"Amara, are you okay? You look upset." He says burping.

"I'm fine." I continue to walk upstairs to my room.

"Who was that man? He doesn't look like a teenager!" He asks.

"Dad, I just can't tonight, okay?. I'm going to bed." I keep walking as he sympathizes with the tiredness in my eyes.

Dear Diary:

The heart will ask no questions and forgive all when it comes to the person you love. Jabari was seconds away from losing the part of him that makes him human. I feel like I'm missing a part of myself being with him, but I have gained as well. The tears I'm crying aren't for Jabari. My tears are of the trust that is now hanging in that between us.

COBALT

~Amara

Hieroglyphs

My drug of choice has become writing. Nothing else has been able to give me great satisfaction. Only a few people understand what that high is like. I decide to take a week off from school. I just need time to process my life and where it's going. This week I have gone through at least five journals. My brain has been unable to shut down, and my fingers are unable to keep still. My homework is done, the house is clean, and dinner is made. There is nothing else for me to do. Jabari and I haven't spoken. He's probably too upset with himself to even say anything to me. At this point, I don't know how to start a conversation with him. There's no easy way he can apologize to me. I just can't let this go either. I know the risk of being with a lion.

It was late in the afternoon when Pharaoh shows up at my house unannounced. I wasn't expecting anyone, so I wasn't adequately dressed for visitors. My pajama pants once green, but now taking on a pastel green color from being faded were old and torn a little at the bottom. I was also wearing a white tank top with a stain above where my belly button is from the spilled coffee I was drinking this morning. I'm assuming that Jabari has gone to school every day this week and saw that I wasn't there. Pharaoh, once again, is the voice of reason between us. He has become the brother I have never had. He was shirtless only wearing jeans and gym shoes. His dreads weren't pulled back as usual. His demeanor was unsettling almost like something terrible has happened.

"Hey, Pharaoh. You know they make this thing called a shirt. What's wrong?" I say letting him in the house.

"Nothing I'm just stopping by to check on you. My family is from African it's scorching hot there. Walking around without clothes on is a normal thing. Plus, we were born without clothing my dear." He says licking his mouth.

"Okay, well, it's Thursday the middle of the afternoon. I'm smart, so I guess Jabari has been at school all week looking for me, and he told you that I have not been there. Which is why you know exactly where I would be. Otherwise, you would have shown up after school to talk to me." I say sitting on the arm of the couch.

"You know you're too smart for your own good." He says.

"So carrier, what's the message you have to deliver?" I say.

"No message. He just wanted me to make sure you are okay." He stands tall in front of me.

"He knows you are here, and I know you guys can read each other's minds. I'm pretty sure he's talking your head off right about now." I look down.

"He's very protective of you. The last thing he or any of us wants is for you to get hurt." He picks up my head from looking down.

"I know. You can tell Jabari, that if he wants to come over and talk I'll allow it." I stand up looking Pharaoh in the eyes.

"Okay. I just told Jabari. My grandfather was right Oya's energy is around you." He says while I walk him to the door.

I locked the door and watch Pharaoh drive away in the window. I glance over at the clock, it was getting close to school being let out for the day. I run upstairs and hop in the shower. I wash, shave, and put on lotion. I fluff out my twists as best as I could. Fluffing them out didn't help at all, my twists were completely flat. There was no other option but to pull my hair back into a high ponytail. My room now was a mess because I couldn't find any of my black leggings. Which is impossible because I own a hundred pair. Quick thinking reminding myself I washed them last week and they were hanging up in the basement. Once I was fully dressed the doorbell rings, which could only be Jabari. Out of breath and now sweaty. I made my way up the stairs and answer the door. He looks like he had been going through hell without seeing me. The guilt was eating him alive. I step outside and close the door behind me.

"Hey, Jabari." I say trying to sound sad.

"Amara, I can't tell you how sorry I am. I never want to hurt you. I don't know what came over me. There are no words that can describe how sorry I am." He says.

"What would you have done if you would have killed me?" I ask folding my arms and trying not to make eye contact.

"I don't know. I would have lost my mind if I had hurt you. I would have probably killed myself." He confesses.

"I don't know what to do from here. I should hate you. Jabari, I should want to tell everyone about you and your family! I can't because I love you too much to do that. You and I are going to heal, but it's going to take some time." I say.

"I promise I will make it up to you. I'm practicing harder on self-control." He says on his knees.

"Practice makes progress." I say giving him a single kiss on his forehead.

Jabari gets up off the floor and looks at me. If I could guess what he was thinking, he's wondering how I could forgive him. He's a Black king who deserves forgiveness from his queen. Even I can show mercy. My fear is making the man I love pay for what my father has done to me. Redemption is all I can say.

I'm still not concerned with my safety around him. In the last five months, he never has put my life in danger. Even when he was about to attack me, he still couldn't bring himself to do so. There is no manual on how to deal with this situation. Somehow, I've adapted myself into the lion's way of living. Jabari telling me that humans can turn into animals allows me to see things from a different perspective. I was curled up on the couch taking a nap when I was peacefully awoken by a couple of soft knocks on the door. I unwrapped myself out of the bulky blanket. I was still sleepy, and couldn't wake up entirely when I got over to the door. Bejeray was here with a huge bag. She looks like the wind had been taken out of her.

"Hey, Amara! Sorry, I know that this is late notice, but I would love to braid your hair." She says.

"Sure." I say moving out the way letting her in.

I sit on the floor in between her legs in my room while she sits on my bed braiding my hair. I couldn't remember the last time someone else braided my hair. It was nice having her hands braid my hair into place. Although I felt like my brain cells were being braided as well.

"Amara, Jabari loves you so much. He is so sorry for what happened to you. I know he told you about Gregory." She says.

"He did. That an extreme pain I can't even imagine." I say.

227

"No one has any idea how horrible I felt and still feel." She says.

"I'm sorry." I say.

"I felt so bad for hurting him. Sometimes I have flashback back to that night. It's a hard pill to swallow. I have put off dating for a couple of years because of it. Until I saw you and Jabari. I found my power when I saw you with him. The look on your face when he comes around is the same look I used to have. Amara, because of you I'm dating a guy named Alexander from the clothing store at the end of the road. I can't thank Jabari enough for bringing you around." She says.

Bejeray finishes up my hair and leaves for the night. She gives me a lot to think about. I guess, in a way, I and Jabari's relationship has given the people around us a bit of hope. The pain Bejeray carried around with her for years is unbearable. Somehow through the darkness, she was able to find her way out. She's stronger than anyone I know. Bejeray is a mighty woman, with a healthy head on her shoulders.

Dear Diary:

I feel like I'm stupid staying with Jabari after he nearly killed me. What is it about him that I can't seem to quit so easily? It almost like he has become my drug, and I'm refusing to go to rehab for my addiction.

It's times like this I miss my mom the most. Even though I wouldn't be able to tell her the whole truth she would be able to give me some guidance. I'm more surprised that I wasn't scared of him. I think I'm just naive and blinded by love. Everything Bejeray said made perfect sense. I understand the life of a lion much more clearly.

~Amara

I'm starting to lose my foundation. In a minute I will have nothing to be able to stand on. I have no family, which is why I believe that I'm becoming so dependent upon Jabari. I have nothing left in me to start over with someone else. Healing doesn't come without pain and suffering. I kept the motto of never making time for someone who won't make time for you. Jabari is making the time for me, so I can't let him go.

Even though I haven't been to school all week, I figured it's Friday, and it wouldn't hurt to go to school one day. I walk to school in such a rush. Mainly because I wanted to hurry up and get the day over with already. As soon as I reach school Zhivago quickly spots me out of a crowd of people.

"Amara! Wait up!" He yells.

"I don't have anything to say to you leave me alone!" I yell walking faster.

"I'm sorry!" He says jumping in front of me.

"You're the last person I want to see right now!" I shout.

"It was a mistake. It won't happen again." He says.

"Leave me alone, Zhivago. This time you have really messed up." I walk away from him.

"Amara, please forgive me!" He says causing a scene.

I walk away from Zhivago pissed. He made a mess out of me and Jabari's relationship. If he only knew the damage he caused. An apology isn't going to help me figure out what I'm going to do. When I arrive at my locker and opened it, letters and candy just pour out of it. I picked up a couple of the notes, they were signed by Jabari. I know he's sorry for what he did. I see the effort he is putting in to try and make things right with us again. I want more than anyone else to be on good terms with him. I love him.

I decide to skip sitting with my friends at lunch and eat by my locker like I used to. I knew that Jabari would see me not sitting with everyone else. He would come and find me, and I was right. I see him walking down the hall. I'm struggling trying not to turn my back on everyone. Our love is like an empire. All of them burn down eventually. It's just a matter of time before your action can catch up with you. Once he was in front of me, a hurricane started forming in my brain.

"Hey, Jabari." I say quietly.

"Hey, Amara." He says.

"I forgive you. I can't find a reason not to. I'm flawed in that way I guess. I have changed so much with being with you. When I'm with you, I see the world differently." I say.

"Your flaws are your best advantage. They are what makes you Amara. When I look at you, I don't see anything wrong with you." He says sitting beside me as I placed my head on his shoulder.

We finish the lunch period just sitting with one another and clearing the air to start afresh. In the last few seconds before the lunch ending bell rings I take a few moments to write in my diary.

Dear Diary:

Showing mercy does not equate to how weak you are. It shows how strong of a person you are.

~Amara

I went home with Jabari after school. Minnie and Issa weren't back yet, it was just the boys. When I entered the house, Sir immediately removed himself from the room. I'm guessing he was really ashamed of himself for what he did. I sit at the table and watch the boys view videos on their phone. It was some guy in a wig doing something silly.

"People are trying to de-masculinize African American men, this stuff is not okay." Dajon says.

"I'm so sick of seeing these brothers in wigs for views." Fayden says.

"Now they're starting to wear women's clothing. Next thing they will be on stripper poles for views." Shamari says leaning over Fayden's shoulder.

"You boys are so naive." I say.

"How?! They're making Black men look bad!" Fayden says stopping the video.

"If putting a wig, lipstick, and women's clothing allows those brothers to eat that should be accepted in the community. It's better for them to make a video with a wig on than to have them on the street selling drugs and being locked up for years because of a drug offense. Let them be in a wig, I promise you those brothers make money doing those videos. They are marketing genius." I say.

I stay for dinner and hang out with everyone. It was nice to see everyone getting along with each other. Sir eventually comes back and apologizes to me. I accept it of course, not wanting to make him feel bad before I left for the night. When Jabari drives me home, I talk to him picking his brain. Even though he won't admit anything to me, I know that he is still dealing with the guilt. I feel guilty waiting so long to accept that he was sorry. He's still new to this. Now if Pharaoh would have done that to me, I would have been way more upset. He's the oldest and has been a lion for years. Out of everyone, he should have the most control, but again they can't help it.

"Jabari, do you want to go hiking with me tomorrow? We can hike to our spot in the woods." I say.

"I would love to do that." He smiles.

I went to bed that night excited about tomorrow. My bed felt softer than ever. I think it was God's way of telling me that everything is going to be okay. He's in control of it all. I was

happy, it was almost like I got a new breath of fresh air.

The Motherland

It was a beautiful day the sun was shining brightly. It was the perfect day for me and Jabari to go hiking. Instead of driving to the woods I ask if we could walk to it. I was happy that Jabari and I were back on good terms. There is no point in holding on to so much hate when there's so much love in the world. The sky was clear and the birds were singing. The world seemed to be at peace. I was delighted, and I don't know what is causing it. I don't think Jabari had anything to do with it. The doorbell rings and I knew it was Jabari ready to go on the hike. I grab my backpack full of water and snacks. Apparently, our minds were working as one today. We both were wearing all black.

"Hey, ready to go?" He asks.

"Yes." I say.

"You know going on a hike is going to be hard work?" He laughs.

"Hard work is never easy. There will be days you're so tired all you could do is sit in silence. It will always be worth it in the end." I say locking the door to my house.

We began walking in the forest. It felt great just being able to walk in the woods. Usually, when we walk through the woods, I'm riding on Jabari's back to our little spot. It has become a place that we can call our own. I walk in front of Jabari moving through the thick trees and mud. I feel happy once we reached our spot. I put my backpack down and change out of my sweats into my swimsuit which was beneath my clothing. I jump into the water and wait for Jabari to join me.

"What has happened to you?" He says.

"Nothing I love life. Come on, jump! Come swim with me! I forgot cats are scared of water." I say splashing him with water

We stays in the woods for a while, just hanging out with each other. We watch the sunset a little before we start to head back. The sunset was the perfect mixture of purple and pink. God is making are hearts smile when the sky changes. Eventually, we made it back to my neighborhood. We were three blocks from my house. I couldn't help but dance a little bit, even though there wasn't any music playing. I was happy and full of life. I snuck a kiss with Jabari while he wasn't looking at me. He looks shocked.

"I love you." I say.

"I love you, too. I'm glad we are working towards being stronger as a couple." He smiles.

"I'm glad that we found each other. I have found my king." I smile.

"I have my queen." He kisses me.

There were a man and a woman dressed in all black that run passed us. I couldn't see their faces, although we didn't pay them any mind and continue to walk. There was a woman just arriving home and was loudly talking on the phone and staring at us. An old man wearing white pajamas comes out of the house with an AR-15 in his hand. I don't believe civilians should have access to military weapons such as these. Out of all the guns in the world, he had to pull out guns that have taken the lives of more people than I can count.

"You two broke into my house! I called the cops!" He yells.

"We didn't! Our hands are up!" Jabari says.

"Don't shoot us! We have our hands up! We are unarmed!" I yell.

"Shut up, you people are going to get arrested. Get a job and stop trying to take things from hard working people!" The man yells.

"You're not listening to us we saw two people run past us. We are just coming back from a hike!" I yell.

"Put the gun down. We are high school seniors and we don't have any weapons on us!" Jabari yells.

The old man missed a step trying to come down the stairs. His hand was still on the trigger. The loud noise of the gun going off was all I can remember. Then I feel it, I'm shot multiple times. I was standing closer to the sidewalk. Jabari was more facing the street. The woman who was talking loud stops talking and was recording the whole thing. It was the worst pain that I have ever experienced. My clothing soaks up my blood.

"Jabari!" I say placing my hand on my chest falling to the ground.

"No, no! Amara!" He screams.

The woman runs over to me trying to help save my life. She must have been a nurse because she seemed to know what she was doing. The police arrive and remove the gun away from the old man. I watch the officer look at me trying to help save my life.

My blood is painting the street a bright shade of red. It was cold, cold enough that I could see the steam in the air evaporating from my blood. I'm lying on the ground with at least six bullet holes accumulating around my body, some of the neighbors come out because of the sound of gunshots. I can barely take a full breath. Jabari is trying to keep me alive, but my eyelids became heavy. I was working so hard to keep my eyes open, but I couldn't. I look up at him wanting to tell him how much I loved him. His tears ran from his cheeks down into his shirt. My breathing slowed down. I'm just like the slaves waiting for a chance to run away to seek their freedom. What some people fail to conclude is the slaves were never freed. They were presented with the illusion of freedom. I have died like a slave given liberty, but not freedom. I'm forever immortalized as an unarmed Black kid killed never to receive justice.

AISHA BUFORD-MORRISON

Advice from the Author

To all the little African boys and girls in improvised

 neighborhoods with a dream, you can do it because I did. Dreams are the most important thing that we have. No one else can make your dreams come alive other than you. Are you willing to put in the work to make your dream a reality? Everyone has a talent. Don't think you have nothing. Everyone has a unique trait. That unique thing is what makes you, you. I wrote two books and I have a learning disability.

The choices you make can move you closer or away from your goals. Keep an eye on your target. You're not living the best of your life until you go after the thing you love the most. Your dreams matter. Stop putting them off. There will always be time. Always remember people who don't have the loudest voices, speak the loudest. The powerless will always have the most power. Your struggles are your greatest gift. Tell them your story!

~Aisha Buford-Morrison

COBALT

www.ingramcontent.com/pod-product-compliance
Lightning Source LLC
Chambersburg PA
CBHW070913180626
46817CB00003B/1046